THE SUDOKU PUZZLE MURDERS

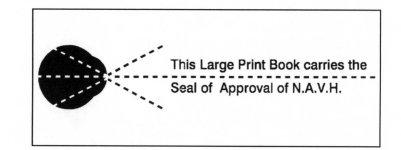

This Large Print Book carries the
Seal of Approval of N.A.V.H.

A PUZZLE LADY MYSTERY

THE SUDOKU PUZZLE MURDERS

PARNELL HALL

THORNDIKE PRESS
A part of Gale, Cengage Learning

GALE
CENGAGE Learning™

Detroit • New York • San Francisco • New Haven, Conn • Waterville, Maine • London

 GALE
CENGAGE Learning

Thorndike Press® Large Print Mystery.
The text of this Large Print edition is unabridged.
Other aspects of the book may vary from the original edition.
Set in 16 pt. Plantin.
Printed on permanent paper.

LIBRARY OF CONGRESS CATALOGING-IN-PUBLICATION DATA

Hall, Parnell.
    The sudoku puzzle murders : a Puzzle Lady mystery / by
Parnell Hall.
        p. cm. — (Thorndike Press large print mystery)
    ISBN-13: 978-1-4104-0864-8 (hardcover : alk. paper)
    ISBN-10: 1-4104-0864-7 (hardcover : alk. paper)
    1. Felton, Cora (Fictitious character) — Fiction. 2. Sudoku —
Fiction. 3. Puzzles — Fiction. 4. Murder — Fiction. 5. Large
type books. I. Title.
PS3558.A37327S63 2008b
813'.547—dc22   2008016076

Published in 2008 by arrangement with St. Martin's Press, LLC.

Printed in the United States of America
1 2 3 4 5 6 7 12 11 10 09 08

For Ruth, who suggested sudoku

WORDS AND NUMBERS

Many of the puzzles in this book are sudoku. The Puzzle Lady had never dealt with number puzzles before, and found it a refreshing change. I, on the other hand, had no idea how to construct them. Luckily, Will Shortz, *New York Times* crossword puzzle editor, NPR puzzle master, star of the movie *Wordplay,* and editor and presenter of his own series of enormously popular sudoku books, had no problem. Will created all the sudoku that appear in this book. I can't thank him enough.

I would also like to thank the versatile Manny Nosowsky for creating both the Puzzle Lady's crossword puzzles and that of the killer. Manny is so adept at fiendish construction that if there was ever an actual crossword puzzle killing, he would be the first person I would suspect. In which case, I would have to inform the police. I hope he understands.

I would also like to thank Ellen Ripstein for editing words and numbers alike. "I'm not particularly good at sudoku," Ellen said, before whipping right through them. I suppose all things are relative. A national champion, Ellen is particularly good with words. She is the true Puzzle Lady.

CHAPTER 1

Cora Felton gripped the black marker firmly in her right hand and stepped up to the easel in the front of the Bakerhaven, Connecticut, town hall. On the white board was a giant square. Thick, black lines in the shape of a tic-tac-toe divided it into nine smaller squares. Thinner black lines divided each in turn into nine even smaller squares. In some of these squares, numerals from 1 through 9 had been entered, one number per square.

A sudoku.

In the back of the crowded town hall, Aaron Grant, just in from the airport, stashed his suitcase behind the door, and scanned the rows of seats for Sherry Carter. She had to be there. Cora Felton, the much vaunted Puzzle Lady, who hawked breakfast cereal to children in TV ads, was merely a figurehead, a kindly, grandmotherly face to adorn the nationally syndicated crossword puzzle column. Sherry actually created the puzzles. Cora could neither construct nor solve a crossword puzzle if her life depended on it. Only a handful of people knew the secret. Cora was always running the risk of being exposed as a fake. Without Sherry, she was lost.

But Cora's niece wasn't there.

Becky Baldwin, easily Bakerhaven's attorney most likely to be mistaken for a Gap dancer, waved him over.

"Where's Sherry?" Aaron whispered, sliding into a seat next to her.

She shrugged. Becky used to date Aaron, and still bristled at the name of her rival.

"She isn't here?"

"Haven't seen her."

"Strange," Aaron said. He wondered how Cora was going to get through. The Puzzle Lady's presentations were usually like a marionette act, with Sherry pulling the strings.

Cora glanced at the board, then back at her audience. "Ladies and gentlemen, for the two percent of you who have never seen one of these, this is a sudoku. For the ten percent of you who don't know how to solve one, I'm going to show you."

Cora turned to the puzzle. She knew exactly how to explain it, because Sherry

				2				8
2		4	6				1	7
		3	8			2		4
7			5					
8					2		9	1
6			9	3		7		
							7	
3		6	7		5	4		
	7	2				1	5	3

had drilled it into her head the night before. "As I'm sure you know, the sudoku is a puzzle in which the numbers one through nine appear once and only once in every row and column. The numbers also appear once and only once in the nine boxes of each three-by-three square." Cora pointed them out. "There are nine three-by-three squares in the puzzle.

"A sudoku starts with some of the numbers filled in." Cora pointed to the blackboard. "This is an easy sudoku. At least, I hope it is, because I'm going to show you how to solve it.

"Look at the three-by-three square in the upper left hand corner. There's a two, a three, and a four in that square. See if you can figure out where to put a seven."

Several hands went up. Someone yelled, "Above the four."

Cora smiled. "I see most of you already know. That's right, a seven goes in the box in the first row across and the third column down. And why does it go there? It can't go in the first column, because there's a seven in the fourth row of that column, and you can't have two sevens in the same column. And it can't go in the second column, because there's a seven in the ninth row of that column. So it must be in the third column. The box in the second row of that column is already filled with a four. The box in the third row is already filled with a three. So the only place it can go is the box in the first row of the third column."

Cora curtsied and gestured in the direction of the person who shouted. "Which is the box above the four.

"Using the same sort of logic, we can figure out where the rest of the numbers go."

Cora quickly filled in the rest of the puzzle. She flashed her trademark Puzzle Lady smile. "And that," she said, "is how you solve a sudoku."

Harvey Beerbaum pushed his way for-

5	6	7	1	2	4	9	3	8
2	8	4	3	6	9	5	1	7
1	9	3	8	5	7	2	6	4
7	3	9	5	4	1	8	2	6
8	4	5	6	7	2	3	9	1
6	2	1	9	3	8	7	4	5
4	5	8	2	1	3	6	7	9
3	1	6	7	9	5	4	8	2
9	7	2	4	8	6	1	5	3

ward. The portly cruciverbalist took the microphone from Cora, flashed her a sly smile. "That's all well and good, Miss Felton. But, as you point out, that's an easy puzzle. Not very challenging to solve. Wouldn't you like to try something harder?"

Cora looked Harvey up and down, rolled her eyes at the audience. "Write your own punch line, gang. I'm afraid to touch that one."

Harvey frowned at the laughter, then blushed furiously. "I mean a more difficult puzzle. A tougher sudoku. A diabolical one."

"That sounds scary, Harvey. I'm not sure these people are up for that."

"What do you think, ladies and gentlemen?" Harvey said. "Wouldn't you like to

see the Puzzle Lady solve a diabolical sudoku?"

The audience applauded.

"Me?" Cora said. "What do you mean,
me? You're the one who suggested it. If
anyone's gonna solve it, it ought to be you."

Another round of applause greeted that
challenge.

"I will if you will," Harvey said.

Cora blinked. "Huh?"

"Why don't we both solve it? At the same
time. In front of everybody. And see who
finishes first?"

Becky nudged Aaron. "Is this part of the
program?"

"No way."

"You think Cora can take him?"

Aaron's smile was forced. Becky didn't
know Sherry was the Puzzle Lady. Without
Sherry, Cora couldn't take him at all.

For the moment, however, Cora was tap
dancing bravely. "I wouldn't want to show
you up, Harvey," she declared, with a
twinkle in her eye.

The townspeople hooted and applauded.

"Oh, I'm not worried," Harvey said. "I've
gotten pretty good at these little number
things."

"He's calling them 'little number things'
for effect," Cora said. "He actually knows

14

they're sudoku. That is how you pronounce it, isn't it, Harvey?"

"You pronounce it very well," Harvey said. "But how fast can you *solve* it?"

"Why? You got an appointment?"

"I actually plan to be here," Harvey said, "for the next twenty minutes or so. Which is as long as it should take me to complete the diabolical puzzle. I don't know about you."

"Ladies and gentlemen," Cora declared, "this is the ultimate of chutzpah. The guy constructs a puzzle, then offers to solve it."

"I assure you I've done nothing of the kind," Harvey said. "I can't believe you'd accuse me of such a thing. I'm suggesting you solve a puzzle constructed by someone else."

"Some friend of yours?" Cora said. "I'm supposed to trust that you haven't had a peek?"

Cora was having a good time ribbing Harvey. There was no reason in the world why she had to accept his outrageous challenge. If she wanted, she could leave him up on-stage solving his own damn diabolical puzzle.

"Oh, I think you'll find the constructor's credentials unimpeachable." Harvey pulled an envelope from his pocket, and took out a letter. He opened it and read, "Dear Harvey. Sorry I couldn't be there in person to help with your charity drive. Please allow me to donate this sudoku. I hope you and the Puzzle Lady have fun solving it."

Harvey looked up from the letter and smiled. "Sincerely, Will Shortz!"

CHAPTER 2

At the excited murmurs that accompanied the announcement, Harvey smiled and nodded triumphantly. "That's right. Will Shortz. Crossword puzzle editor of the *New York Times* and star of the movie, *Wordplay.*"

Harvey held up another envelope. "Will's letter came with this enclosure. A sealed envelope, containing the sudoku for the Puzzle Lady and me to solve. What do you think of that?"

The audience answered with applause.

"Uh, oh," Aaron said.

"What's the matter?" Becky whispered.

"That's just like Harvey. Issuing a public challenge without asking if it's okay first."

"Can she say no?"

"With Will Shortz donating a puzzle? Not a chance."

Behind her frozen smile, Cora glared daggers at Harvey Beerbaum, as he bustled around the stage, setting up two sudoku grids side by side. Cora had brought only one for her lecture, but Harvey, maddeningly prepared, had brought another.

Harvey the curmudgeon, having completely usurped Cora's demonstration, danced around like a frenetic movie director. "We need impartial people to set up the sudoku. And who could be more impartial than our own chief of police, Dale Harper. And our own first selectman, Iris Cooper. Iris, Chief, could you come up here and supervise our proceedings?"

Chief Harper, who'd been sitting with his wife and daughter, got reluctantly to his feet, and pressed forward with all the enthusiasm of a man on his way to the gallows.

First selectman Iris Cooper, who had no idea she was going to be called on, looked to Cora for guidance. The Puzzle Lady merely rolled her eyes.

"Here you are, Chief, Ms. Cooper. If you would take these black markers. And while Cora and I look away. You will, won't you, Cora?"

"Are you accusing me of cheating, Harvey? I may have cheated on a husband or two, but I never cheat at sudoku."

"So, Chief, Ms. Cooper. If you would please copy the numbers onto these two giant sudoku. Let me know when you're done."

Cora and Harvey stood facing the audience. Behind them, Chief Harper and Iris Cooper worked on the puzzles.

"Can we bet on *them?*" Cora grinned. "Ten bucks says Iris beats the chief."

"Hey, I resent that," Chief Harper said.

"So bet on yourself," Cora told him.

"Fat chance," Iris scoffed. "He's way behind."

When the puzzles were done, Harvey asked the audience, "Are they the same?"

"Yes."

"Fine. Cora, would you like to turn around?"

"I think you have to marry me before you start suggesting positions," Cora said wickedly. She looked, whistled. "Wow! That's a killer sudoku puzzle."

"Uh, no," Harvey said pedantically. "Actually, the killer sudoku puzzle is the one where the numbers in adjoining squares have been added together —"

"Good lord, Harvey," Cora scoffed. "You're way too literal. By killer puzzle I mean it's diabolical. Very hard. Not easy to do. Anyone out there confused by what I just said?"

A shaking of heads and chorus of noes.

19

```
┌───────┬───────┬───────┐
│ 1 · · │ · 7 3 │ · · · │
│ · 9 · │ 4 · · │ · · · │
│ · · · │ · 6 · │ · · 8 │
├───────┼───────┼───────┤
│ · 2 · │ · · · │ · 6 · │
│ · · · │ · 1 · │ · · · │
│ · 5 4 │ · · · │ 8 · 7 │
├───────┼───────┼───────┤
│ 9 · · │ · 8 · │ · 7 · │
│ · 3 · │ · · · │ · · 9 │
│ · · 5 │ 9 4 · │ 2 · · │
└───────┴───────┴───────┘
```

"No one," Cora said. "Just the expert. We get the picture, Harvey. This is one tough puzzle. You, I take it, can solve it."

"Of course I can solve it. The only question is can I solve it as fast as you can."

"I'm sure you can, Harvey. You're a man. You can do anything better than a woman. Isn't that right?"

Harvey looked aghast. "No. Of course not."

"Relax, Harvey. You're a sexist pig and we love you. So, you think a woman can't beat a man?"

"I never said any such thing. I merely meant we could have a race. As fellow constructors. Sex has nothing to do with it."

"Trust me, Harvey, sex *always* has something to do with it. Anyway, before you went off on a tangent about how men are better than women, you were telling us what was going to happen."

"I was just explaining the rules."

"Rules? In a knife fight?"

Harvey frowned.

"It's from *Butch Cassidy and the Sundance Kid.*"

"I don't know it."

"Obviously not, or you wouldn't be standing so straight. Right after that line, Paul Newman kicks the guy in the crotch."

Becky nudged Aaron. "Is she stalling?"

"She's just having fun with him. To pay him back for trying to embarrass her with the surprise contest."

"In other words, she's stalling?"

Aaron grimaced. Figured he'd better pave the way for Cora's failure. "I'm not sure how good she is at solving sudoku. They're not the same as crossword puzzles."

"Uh, oh," Becky said.

"You're right," Harvey said. "No rules. We each have a sudoku to solve. Whoever solves it first wins. Now, Chief, if you and Ms. Cooper would just take those two large sudoku and tilt the outer edges toward the back wall. How's that, Cora? Now you can't

21

see mine, and I can't see yours."

Cora put her hand to her head. "Please, Harvey, don't give me straight lines like that."

The crowd roared.

Harvey blushed, then forged ahead. "All right. No rules. We just start solving. First one with the correct solution. Ready. Set. Go!"

Harvey turned around, studied his sudoku.

Cora studied hers. She took the microphone. "My goodness. You know, Will Shortz may be a great constructor, but he's left a lot of numbers out. This would be much easier to solve with more squares filled in."

Harvey, oblivious, continued working on his puzzle.

"You mind if I call Will Shortz, ask him for some more numbers?" Cora nodded to the audience. "I'll take that as a yes. Anyone got a cell phone?"

"I do," Iris said.

"Thanks." Cora took the phone, punched in an arbitrary number, pretended to talk to Will Shortz. "Hello, Will? . . . Cora Felton . . . Yeah, hi . . . I'm working on your killer sudoku puzzle." She listened, rolled her eyes. "Yes, I *know* it's not a 'killer' sudoku puzzle . . . Why am I calling? Oh.

About your puzzle . . . Well, it's rather hard. I was wondering if you could help me with the numbers? . . . Huh? . . . Thanks, Will."

Cora flipped the cell phone closed, handed it back to Iris.

"Hey, Harvey!" Cora called.

Harvey, deep in thought, took awhile to react. "What?"

"I was just on the phone with Will Shortz. He gave me some help with the puzzle. I think it's only fair I share it with you."

"What are you talking about?"

"I told him the puzzle was too hard, so he gave me a number."

Harvey frowned. "What number?"

Cora smiled innocently. "Three."

"Three?"

"Yes."

"Okay. So where does the number three go?"

"Oh. He didn't tell me that," Cora said. "But, trust me, there's a three in the puzzle."

Harvey stared at her. Blinked.

A ripple of laughter spread though the town hall as the audience slowly realized Cora was putting him on.

Cora shook her head. "No sense of humor. He seems to be doing pretty well with the puzzle, though."

Harvey was.

"He's more than half done," Becky whispered to Aaron.

"Yeah."

"What's she doing? Is this like a chess tournament where one player lets the clock run to try to psych their opponent out?"

"I have no idea," Aaron said. He was speculating wildly on what excuses Cora might come up with for not being about to solve the puzzle.

"Ah, you're no fun, Harvey." Cora picked up the marker and began writing numbers at an astounding rate. Within minutes she had filled the board. "Done!" she announced.

The crowd burst into applause.

Harvey, startled, looked around in sur-

1	8	6	2	7	3	5	9	4
2	9	7	4	5	8	6	3	1
5	4	3	1	6	9	7	2	8
7	2	1	8	3	4	9	6	5
8	6	9	5	1	7	3	4	2
3	5	4	6	9	2	8	1	7
9	1	2	3	8	5	4	7	6
4	3	8	7	2	6	1	5	9
6	7	5	9	4	1	2	8	3

prise. He was nearly three quarters done.

Cora winked at him. "You just ain't ready for me yet, kid."

Harvey gawked.

"*Cincinnati Kid,* Harvey. Steve McQueen. Rent it some time."

Cora set down her marker, curtsied to the crowd, and walked out.

CHAPTER 3

Cora Felton stood in the parking lot behind town hall smoking a cigarette.

"You mind telling me how you pulled that off?" Aaron Grant said.

"Oh, hi, Aaron. You got back in time to see my performance?"

"I sure did. How the hell did you do it?"

"Do what?"

"Solve the sudoku?"

"Weren't you listening? You put nine numbers in each row and column."

"I know the concept."

"There you are." Cora took a drag on her cigarette, blew it out.

"But you can't do puzzles."

"Says who?"

"Says you. You're terrible at puzzles."

"Shhh. You never know who might be listening."

"Come on. Were you and Harvey in on it?"

"In on what? The guy surprised me onstage. He tried to trip me up. Just like he always tries to do."

"Right. With a sealed puzzle from Will Shortz. So how'd you get a look at the puzzle?"

"Harvey opened the envelope and gave it to me."

"I mean beforehand."

"What do you care, Aaron? You can't print this."

"I'm marrying into the family. If your niece has powers of ESP, I'd like to know about it."

"You think Sherry helped me solve the puzzle?"

"Well, didn't she?"

Cora smiled. "Sherry's bad at sudoku."

"What?"

"It's all math. There's no words for her to wrap her torturous mind around. I, on the other hand, love sudoku for just that reason. No damn words. No clues with double meanings. Just numbers. They're either right or they're wrong."

"You mean . . . ?"

"I'm a whiz at sudoku. I beat Harvey fair and square. I could beat most men on the eastern seaboard. You can't believe what a relief it is to actually *have* an expertise I profess."

"So where's Sherry?"

"She got a little behind in her work. I'm not sure why. Something about a wedding."

"Uh huh." Aaron absently pushed gravel with his foot. "Dennis been around?"

"Aaron."

"Hey, I'm out of town, I worry. The guy won't leave her alone."

"And neither will you. I swear to God, I don't know which one of you agitates her more."

"Then he's been here?"

"I haven't seen him. Sherry hasn't mentioned him. That's all I know."

"She hasn't mentioned him?"

"No, and if you're smart, you won't either."

Aaron sighed. "Okay. Tell her I'll call her from the paper."

"You're going to work?"

"I gotta write a puff piece on your presentation." He shrugged. "Thanks to Harvey, it will be a little more interesting."

Cora watched Aaron go, took a drag on her cigarette. What would it be like to have a newsman as an in-law? Aaron was a good guy, but even so. Some of the nicest people in the world became absolute gorgons once you married into their families. Husbands included.

"Miss Felton?"

Cora looked up in annoyance to see who had interrupted her train of thought. Her expression immediately changed. The gentleman was quite striking. He was a young Asian man, not tall, but solidly built. He wore slacks, a blue blazer, and a white shirt, open at the neck, which, on a Sunday afternoon, made him better dressed than most of Bakerhaven. He was clean-shaven, his gleaming black hair was razor-cut. A scar on his left cheek from his lip to his chin didn't detract from his appeal, merely gave him character.

To a woman who had not been married in awhile, he looked awfully good. Cora felt that old tingling sensation. She was almost embarrassed to be caught smoking, considered stamping out her cigarette. Instead, she mustered up her trademark Puzzle Lady smile, weighed possible responses to the gentleman's query. Prudently opted for the single word, "Yes."

He hurried up and took her hand. "I am so pleased to meet you. I am Hideki Taki-yama. I am a great admirer of the Puzzle Lady."

"Are you really?" Cora practically simpered, then reined herself in. Her niece was always warning her to find out who they were before she showed her true colors. "You're not from around here."

"No. I am from Japan."

"Oh. That's a tough commute."

He smiled. "Yes."

Cora sized him up. "Listen, Hideki, if you came all the way from Japan to hear me speak, that's a little scary."

"I am sorry to disappoint you. I am in New York on business. It is not nearly so far."

His English was excellent. Cora wondered if she should tell him so, or whether that would be offensive. It occurred to her life had been easier when she was drinking. She said whatever the hell she felt like, and never worried about the consequences. Of course, she sometimes wound up married.

"I am sorry that I cannot say I came around the world to find you. But in a way I did. I have heard of you in Japan, of course. We get American television. I have seen your excellent advertisements for breakfast cereal."

Cora shuddered at the thought. She covered by pretending to blush.

"But please. Let me tell you how much I enjoyed your presentation. And the ease with which you defeated that man." He leaned in confidentially. "Was that pre-arranged?"

"Lord, no. Harvey is always trying to ambush me in one way or another. He probably practiced all week and figured I didn't."

"But you triumphed easily. Even after giving him the lead."

Cora shrugged. "I have a knack for sudoku. Don't ask me why."

His eyes widened. "But you are the Puzzle Lady."

"Yeah, yeah. Doesn't mean I'm the fastest thing on two wheels." At his confused expression, Cora said, "I'm not sure what that means myself. To be honest, I can't solve crossword puzzles nearly as quickly."

"Interesting."

"Why?"

He frowned. "What?"

"Why is it interesting? Why did you drive all the way from New York to see me?"

"I am sorry." He took out a business card, handed it to Cora. "I am a publisher. Takiyama Publishing is third largest house in Japan. Fiction and nonfiction. We do mystery, romance, science fiction. Sudoku are most popular. I would love to do a Puzzle Lady sudoku book."

"You want to put me in a book?"

"Do you know how big you are in Japan?"

That tripped her up. How big she was in Japan? What a touchy subject. Cora had put on ten pounds in the last two months. Not the end of the world, still nothing she wanted to be reminded of. Of course, Mr. Fujifilm wasn't making a comment on her girth. He was far too polite to do that. He was clearly referring to her celebrity status. On the other hand, Asian women tended to be small and slim, and what was fair about that? Oh, hell, was there anything she could say that didn't sound irritated, off-putting, or couched in an offensive racial stereotype?

Hideki misunderstood her hesitation. "I am sorry to speak business with you. Is it not done? Should I be speaking with your agent?"

"Actually, I don't have an agent."

"Is that so? You do it all yourself? How extraordinary."

"My niece Sherry Carter handles my business affairs. She's not my agent. More like a partnership."

"I see. So I should talk to Miss Carter?"

Cora grimaced. "Miss Carter has wedding plans just now."

"Oh? And when is the happy event?"

Cora waggled her hand. "The date's not set yet. Some trouble with her former husband."

"The divorce is not final?"

"He doesn't think it is."

"Does she have a good lawyer?"

"Her husband does."

He frowned, uncomprehending.

"His lawyer is my lawyer," Cora explained. "An excellent lawyer. But she used to date the groom."

"The present groom?"

"Yes. Now she is the attorney for my niece's ex-husband."

"I see."

Cora judged from his expression he probably didn't. She smiled, said, "No matter. Here's Sherry's number. I'll tell her you're going to call."

Cora fished a handful of assorted papers from her floppy drawstring purse, riffled through, came up with an Exxon receipt. Surely her tax man didn't need that. After all, he had her credit card statements. At least she hoped he did. Cora scrawled the number with a rather blunt pencil, recalled too late as always Sherry urging her to get business cards. Maybe next time.

"Here. Call her later this afternoon. After I get a chance to talk to her."

"You will tell her about me?"

Cora smiled. "Count on it."

CHAPTER 4

Sherry Carter was at the computer, typing a puzzle into Crossword Compiler. Sherry was a little behind in her work, which was why she'd skipped Cora's sudoku presentation. That and her desire to let Cora fly on her own. Any Puzzle Lady appearance that didn't involve Sherry was a godsend. Cora was good at bluffing her way through luncheon talks where no cruciverbal skills were required, but a chance of displaying actual expertise was too good to be true. Cora couldn't solve a *TV Guide* puzzle with a pencil, two erasers, and an answer sheet. But she was an absolute whiz at sudoku. Something clicked in that loopy mind of hers, that miswired mare's nest of nerves and impulse centers, which allowed her to make near miraculous deductions concerning motivations, inclinations, and cause and effect, just as long as it didn't involve defining words. And intersecting words. And fitting words into five-letter blanks. And knowing whether a word was being used as a noun or a verb. Cora hated nouns and verbs. At least, she hated identifying them, classifying them, and saying how they were used in a sentence. Her teacher tried to drum that into her head in high school, just at the time she was becoming very interested in nonverbal activities.

Cora's language skills had suffered. Not that it had harmed her any. None of the many men she'd married had ever asked her to parse a sentence.

Sherry needed a good clue for *profligate.* Not to be confused with *prodigal.* Which she would never do unless distracted by an upcoming wedding. Good lord. If marriage addled her brain, maybe it wasn't worth it. Maybe they should call the whole thing off.

The phone rang.

Sherry scowled. She hated phone calls when she was constructing. She decided to let the answering machine pick up. Unless it was Cora or Aaron. Sherry checked the caller ID. Damn. *Caller unknown.* That could be anything, from an unlisted number, to a pay phone, to a telemarketer. Oh, well, if it was the last, she could just hang up. But what if it was someone really annoying? Like her ex-husband? Or her ex-husband's wife?

Or her ex-husband's father-in-law, for that matter?

Sherry frowned, snatched up the phone. "Hello?"

"Sherry. Thank God you picked up. I was afraid you'd think I was a crank."

"You are a crank, Cora. Why don't you get a cell phone?"

"I'd lose it. I'd let the battery run down. It would ring in a movie theater or a church."

"When was the last time you were in church?"

"I don't know. I suppose I must have been getting married."

"You can leave a cell phone off, Cora. Only turn it on when you need it."

"It could still get lost."

"So put it in your purse."

"You know what my purse is like? I'd have to empty it out every time I wanted to find the damn thing. It's embarrassing, dragging out six different kinds of birth control."

"Why do you have six different kinds of birth control?"

"Do I have any kids? I've never even been pregnant. Except to force a proposal out of the guy who was terminally shy."

"You were pregnant?"

"No, I just said I was. The guy was too

timid to question my finding."

"Cora, why did you call?"

"To tell you how well it went."

"It did."

"I'll say. Aaron was there and I knocked his socks off."

"Aaron's back?"

"Yeah. He came right from the airport."

"He didn't call."

"He will. He went back to the paper to file his story. Anyway, he didn't know I could solve sudoku. He thought Harvey was going to hang me out to dry."

"Harvey?"

"Yeah. He surprised me with a puzzle from Will Shortz and challenged me to a fight."

"How did that go?"

"I kicked his ass. Anyway, that's not why I'm calling."

"You wanna run through three or four more topics before you tell me?"

"You're rather testy. Prewedding jitters."

"That's one topic."

"That's a *lot* of topics. That's Aaron. And Dennis. And Brenda. And Becky. And Reverend What's-his-face."

"Kimble."

"Yeah, him. Listen, has Dennis been around lately?"

"Why?"

"Why? Well, there's a restraining order, for one thing."

"I mean, why are you asking?"

"To find out if he *has!* Jesus, you and Aaron are impossible!"

"Aaron? Has he been asking?"

"He hasn't even *been* here. Forget Aaron. Just listen a minute."

"I really have to do this puzzle."

"Right. Because you're the brain trust, and I'm just the pretty face. Well, guess what? I got a job I can actually do."

"What's that?"

Cora filled her niece in on the sudoku book.

Sherry was skeptical at best. "A Japanese publisher wants *you* to do a Puzzle Lady book?"

"Yeah. Of sudoku. Is that a problem?"

"Not for me. I can't do the damn things."

"Well, I can."

"Can you construct them?"

"How hard can it be? You plug in nine numbers and take some of them out."

"I think there's more to it than that."

"Yeah, well, the guy's gonna call you to make a deal. I told him you're my business agent."

"Wonderful. Any terms in particular you'd

like me to negotiate?"

"I want a camper, a driver, and a chance to direct."

"It's a book, not a movie."

"Oh, well. Do the best you can."

It took Sherry awhile to get back into the puzzle. She just couldn't concentrate. It bothered her that Aaron hadn't called. She wondered if she should call him at the paper. No, he'd said he'd call her. She didn't want to bother him at work.

Bother. That was all wrong. She wasn't a bother. She was the woman he was going to marry. A call from her could never be a bother.

Sherry went to the phone, picked it up.

Even so.

There was no reason to be obsessive.

Sherry put the phone down again.

Told herself it wasn't just that she didn't want to give him a chance to ask if she'd heard from Dennis.

Sherry put it out of her mind, attacked the puzzle.

She was nearly finished by the time the phone finally rang.

CHAPTER 5

Chief Harper was cleaning out his garage. He'd been meaning to do it for months. Actually, his *wife* had been meaning for him to do it for months. He'd been putting it off. Cleaning out the garage never pleased him the way it pleased her. He was not happy to see the assortment of junk the family had amassed since the last time his wife had prevailed upon him to do it. Nor was he happy with the inevitable tag sale that followed each cleaning. Clara's bike with training wheels would always have a special significance for him. Even when she went off and got married. And wouldn't it be a wonderful thing to give to *her* daughter? Granted, the tires were flat and the kickstand was missing, but you didn't *need* a kickstand with training wheels. And that rust would surely clean right off with WD-40.

Oh! There was a set of old golf clubs. The

ones he'd stored in the garage when he got that new set that seemed way too big to hit such a small ball. But that's how they all played nowadays. To be fair, the new clubs were pretty nice. But they didn't have a pitching wedge, just a sand wedge. And he'd managed to lose his eight iron somewhere on the back nine. Why someone hadn't found it and turned it in was a matter for a police investigation. At any rate, his new clubs were an eight iron and a pitching wedge down, and he always snuck them out of the old bag when he went golfing. He wondered dispiritedly how much his clubs would sell for without them.

Then there was the croquet set with the coat hanger for a hoop. And the lawn mower that still worked but didn't start very often. And the scrap wood that wouldn't have taken up so much room if it were piled neatly. And the living room rug his wife had made him save for just such an occasion. If he dragged it outside it would probably rain. If he didn't drag it outside, he couldn't get at the storm windows behind it.

Chief Harper was in a foul mood by the time he wrestled the rug outside to find Cora Felton standing in his drive.

"What do you want?" Harper snarled.

"Whoa, Chief. Whatever's buggin' you, I

didn't do it."

"What brings you here? Want to buy a rug?"

"Sorry, Chief. Police business. But if you're busy. . . ."

Harper put up his hand. "Actually, I could take a break. What's on your mind?"

"I'm interested in someone."

"Who?"

"The Japanese gentleman who was at my talk at town hall."

Harper smiled. "It's a sad commentary on our diversity that you can describe him as such."

"I'm broken up. Did you see him?"

"I was distracted. My wife was going on about cleaning the garage." Harper stole a guilty glance over his shoulder for fear she was standing there.

"Listen, can you run the guy for me?"

"Run him?"

"Do I have to translate police lingo? Check him out. See if he's got a record."

"In Japan?"

"If that's where he's from. Guy shows up, says he's from Japan. How should I know?"

"Did he look like he was from Japan?"

"He looked damn good. Lean, hard, muscular." Cora noticed the expression on Chief Harper's face, hurried on. "I'd like to know if he's legit."

"Why?"

"He wants to put me in a book."

"A book?"

"Yeah. Of sudoku."

"He wants to publish a book of your puzzles? The man is clearly a scoundrel. Shall I put him under arrest?"

"Fine, make fun," Cora said. "But I don't want to get involved in a business venture with someone who isn't kosher. Particularly someone from another country who I can't get ahold of if I want to wring his neck."

Harper frowned. "This doesn't sound like you, Cora. Investigating a business deal. That's not your style."

"What's my style?"

"Oh, rushing in headlong without looking where you're going, then escaping un-scathed when you get into trouble."

"That flowed trippingly off the tongue, Chief. Can I assume you didn't just make that up?"

Harper raised his hand. "I was explaining to someone why I hadn't arrested you as a public nuisance. I forget who. But it seemed to do the trick."

"You couldn't just say I'd been a big help to you?"

"Right, right," Chief Harper said. "That's

how I like to portray myself. Totally incompetent without you."

"Can you run the name?"

"What is it?"

Cora read Hideki's name off the card.

"Sounds Japanese."

Cora gave him a look.

"All right, I'll run it when I get in tomorrow. Think you can stay out of trouble till then?"

"Think you'll be done with your garage by then?"

"You want that name run or not?"

"Please."

Cora gave Chief Harper the business card.

A police car pulled up and Dan Finley got out. The young officer was a Puzzle Lady fan. He smiled and waved when he saw Cora.

"Hi, Chief. I couldn't get you on the phone."

"Yeah. 'Cause I was in the garage."

"Couldn't get you on the radio, either."

"Probably 'cause it's not on. I'm off duty, Dan."

"Sorry, Chief. Thought you'd want to know."

"Know what?"

"There's been a murder."

CHAPTER 6

Dr. Barney Nathan, dapper as ever in his red bow tie, rose from the body and declared, "This man is dead."

That came as no surprise. The gentleman in question had half his head missing. The left half, Cora observed from her vantage point just behind Chief Harper. Cora had a healthy way of looking at corpses, treating them as puzzles to be solved, rather than human beings on whom gruesome, painful, and, ultimately, deadly things had been done.

The mystery in this case was where the hell was the gentleman's right eye? A gory mass of bone, tissue, and brain that marked the spot where it should have been, offered no immediate clue. Had someone laid the man down and bashed his head in with a rock? Not likely. Then the missing features would be present, if altered. These gave the impression of having been sliced away.

Whether by a pickax, or a chain saw, or . . .

Cora found there might be a small flaw in her philosophy of distancing herself from the carnage. She felt most decidedly light-headed, if not queasy. She steeled herself, hoped Chief Harper wouldn't notice.

He didn't. The chief, pretty much in the same boat, was steadying wobbling knees. He kept his eyes on the doctor rather than the corpse, said, "Can you give me a little more than that, Barney?"

The dapper doctor might have been speaking at a physicians luncheon. "Certainly. The decedent has been dead at least twelve hours. Killed by a blow to the head with some sharp object, most likely not here."

"How can you tell?"

"The gentleman is missing half his face. If the fatal blow had been struck here, you would expect to see some evidence of it. But that's really your department, isn't it?"

"Who is he?"

"I don't know. That's also your department. I would say he was around forty-five or fifty, five-foot-eight, a hundred and sixty pounds. Give or take part of his head."

"You thinking of doing stand-up, Doc?"

Barney frowned, lowered his voice. "Frankly, I'm a little giddy looking at the damn thing."

"Not a pleasant sight, that's for sure," Harper said. "All right, let me check for ID, you can get him down to the morgue."

"Sure."

Chief Harper looked at the body, hesitated. "Dan?"

"What?"

"You want to see if he's got a wallet?"

"Oh."

Clearly no one wanted to go near the corpse. Cora considered volunteering. She was afraid she'd lose her lunch. In front of the medical examiner and the police. She'd never live it down.

Dan approached the body. The dead man wore a sports jacket and slacks. Dan pushed the jacket aside, found a wallet in the hip pocket of the pants.

"His name's Walter Krebb. From New York City. At least according to his driver's license. Assuming it's him."

"Isn't there a photo?"

"Yeah, but . . ."

Harper put up his hand. "Okay, okay. Anything else?"

Dan gave the body a once-over. "He's got something in his jacket pocket."

"Please tell me it's not a crossword puzzle."

"No. It's a — Well, actually."

"Damn it, Dan!"

"It's a newspaper. One of the smaller New York papers. The *New York Star.* Folded open to the puzzle page."

"That *can't* mean anything. Can it?"

"No. Except it's her puzzle."

"Huh?"

"It's a Puzzle Lady puzzle. See, Chief?"

Dan held it up. The newspaper had two puzzles on the page.

One was a sudoku.

The other bore Cora Felton's smiling face. The copy read: *The Puzzle Lady has some advice in case an unexpected guest drops in for dinner.*

Across

1. Frank of the Mothers of Invention
6. What a star may stand for
11. "Proved!" letters
14. Hunter in the sky
15. Spiked, as punch
16. "Eewww, gross!"

17. Advice part 1
19. Prior to now
20. Slam-dance
21. Abbr. on a telephone
22. Cockeyed
24. Results in
26. Takes the plunge?
27. "Sit down and have _____!"
31. Desdemona's love, in opera
33. Advice part 2
35. Add fizz to
39. Enters, as a controversy
40. Attitudes
41. They happen
42. Advice part 3
43. Gooey treat
45. Oneness
46. Bill of Rights defenders: Abbr.
49. How a telegrapher went once
51. "The Sound of Music" name
53. Rural water source
54. Slangy beliefs
58. Chip off the old pot?
59. Advice end
62. Evolution figure
63. Former hurler Ryan
64. Piccolo cousin
65. Cowboy sobriquet
66. "_____ never believe me!"
67. Reason

Down

1. Kind of lens
2. It flows through Florence
3. Thanksgiving desserts
4. Swanky
5. Member of a small colony
6. Put in one's place
7. Acquires a liking for
8. Build up
9. Leaves in a bag?
10. "Giant" author Ferber
11. Big shaker-upper
12. Encouraged, with "on"
13. Graceful craft in the Persian Gulf
18. Forever and a day, seemingly
23. Under oath
24. 1974 hit subtitled "Touch the Wind"
25. Aristotle's teacher
27. ". . . even _____ speak"
28. Young Cleaver, familiarly
29. Third planet from die Sonne
30. Ties
32. React to a surprise, perhaps
34. Old-fashioned denial
36. When Romeo meets Juliet
37. German: Abbr.
38. Catch sight of
40. _____ pony

42. New Jersey resort
44. Shilly-shally
46. Trip to the plate
47. Thin flapjack
48. Paint base
50. Having a high pH: Abbr.
52. Huff or puff
54. Dot of land
55. Flabbergast
56. 2000 pennant winners
57. _____' Pea
60. Kabuki alternative
61. Failing grades

		1			5		3	9
				6				2
				2				
	8		6	3		5		
4								
5	6	2						
			8	7			5	
						2	1	
		3				7	6	

"Oh, hell," Chief Harper said. "Cora?"

"Yes?"

"Does this mean anything?"

"How the hell should I know?"

"Well, you wrote it, didn't you?"

Uh-oh. There it was, the direct question. Luckily, Cora had been evading direct questions all her life. "You think I know what the answer is? All the crossword puzzles I've ever seen? You think I remember this?"

"Okay, so solve it."

"Oh, sure. Throw a bloody corpse in my lap and ask me to solve a puzzle. A puzzle that's got nothing to do with anything. If the guy had a puzzle pinned to his chest by a knife in his heart, okay, it would be another story. But a puzzle from a paper?

53

Come on."

"I'd still like it solved."

"Fine. Give me the paper. I'll fill it in at home."

"It's evidence."

"Of what? The guy's reading habits? You wanna give it to me, I'll solve it. You don't, that's okay too."

"You want me to Xerox it?" Dan Finley offered.

"Good idea," Harper said. "The puzzle and the sudoku."

"You want me to solve the sudoku too?" Cora said.

"Why not?"

"It doesn't mean anything."

"Then it can't hurt."

Dan Finley went off to photocopy the puzzle. Cora took the opportunity to inspect the crime scene. The body had been found in the back lot of the abandoned Tastee Freez, closed up ever since the Dairy Queen opened a half a mile closer to town and ran them out of business. If the owner of the Tastee Freez had killed the owner of the Dairy Queen, Cora wouldn't have been surprised. But this wasn't him.

Harper wandered over to Cora, said, "See anything?"

"You're asking for my help?"

"A little louder, Cora. I don't think the EMT guys heard you."

"For what it's worth, Chief, the corpse is not from town. According to the doc, he wasn't killed here. So the killer's probably not from town either. Everything points to the fact the guy was killed elsewhere, someone drove through town and dumped the body. If that's true, your sole responsibility will be getting the case into the hands of the proper authorities."

"Uh-huh. And just who would that be?"

Cora waggled her hand. "That's the only problem."

CHAPTER 7

Aaron Grant was out back cooking burgers when Cora got home.

"Ah, the intrepid newsman. Nothing can stay him from his appointed task."

Aaron looked up from the grill. "Cora? Have you been drinking?"

Which wouldn't have been so bad if his face hadn't done a 180, trying to choke back the words. "I mean, what are you talking about?"

"It's all right," Cora said. "I quit drinking, everybody *knows* I quit drinking, it's no big *deal* I quit drinking, and, no, I haven't been drinking. I'm very glad to see you're cooking burgers. I love burgers."

"And what's the bit about me not being swayed from my task?"

"If I tell you, do you promise to keep cooking burgers?"

"Cora."

"There's been a murder."

"What!"

"No big deal," Cora said. "Some guy from New York City got killed and dumped behind the Tastee Freez."

Aaron put down his spatula. "I gotta go cover this."

"No, you don't. Pick that up. I let the air out of your tires. You're not going anywhere."

"You what?!"

"All right, I didn't. But I might as well have. It's a small story. The paper's not going to get out an extra. You got plenty of time to write this up after dinner."

"They're doing the layout now."

"So, call your editor, tell him to hold you two columns on the bottom of the front page."

"He'll want me to come in."

"You can't come in. You're out getting the story."

"Exactly. That's where I need to be right now."

"No, you don't. I got the story. You better flip that one. I like them medium rare."

"I need all the details. The guy's name and address. How he died."

"He had his face bashed in."

"What?"

"I got it all in my purse. Keep cooking.

I'll dig it out for you."

Cora hurried into the house, flopped her purse down on the kitchen table. She wrenched the phone off the wall, punched in a number. "Chief, Cora. Help me out here. I need the dead guy's name and address."

"What for?"

"The newspaper."

"You're writing for the newspaper?"

"No, but I'm hungry."

"What?"

"Aaron's cooking, and I don't want him to stop."

"Aaron's cooking?"

"Barbecuing. You ever barbecue, Chief? Come on, give me the name before he burns my damn burger."

"It's Walter something. Didn't you write it down?"

"I need the address."

Cora hung up the phone just as her niece came into the kitchen. Sherry looked entirely too young, fresh, and perky for her own good. Truly, youth was wasted on the young. With looks like that, Cora could have piled up even more ex-husbands than the ones in whose alimony she reveled.

"Well, he called," Sherry said.

"Who?"

"The Japanese publisher. He sounded very nice. I'm meeting him at the Country Kitchen to discuss a deal."

"When?"

"Tonight."

"Aaron's cooking burgers."

"I'm not meeting him for dinner. Just a drink."

"Does Aaron know you're going out for a drink with a handsome young business-man?"

"Yeah, right," Sherry scoffed.

"What's that supposed to mean?"

"How young is young?"

"Well, he's too old for you. I'm sure he won't see it that way."

"And he's too young for you?"

"Bite your tongue."

"It's not a date, Cora. The guy was only interested in whether I had your power of attorney."

"Do you?"

"You're hopeless. Do you know how much Puzzle Lady business I handle for you?"

"All of it. It's your own business."

"Yeah, but no one knows that. So I need your power of attorney. So I can cash the checks that are made out to you that are really for me."

"You're giving me a headache. Look, do

me a favor. Go out and make sure your boyfriend doesn't burn the food. I made the mistake of telling him someone got killed. Now he wants to cover the story."

"That's his job."

"You wanna take over cooking?"

"I'm meeting a publisher. Why don't you cook?"

"I can't cook."

"You've been married umpteen times and you can't cook?"

"Trust me, none of my husbands married me for my cooking."

"Yeah. Well, I gotta get dressed."

Sherry went down the hall into the bathroom.

The phone rang.

Cora scooped it up. "Hello?"

Hideki Takiyama's voice said, "Sherry Carter?"

"No. Cora Felton. How are you, Hideki?"

"I am fine. I am calling to speak to Miss Carter."

"She's getting dressed. Can it wait till you see her?"

"Wait till I see her?"

"She can't come to the phone right now. Are you calling to say you can't make it?"

"No. Not at all."

"Fine. She'll see you later." Cora hung up

the phone.

Sherry came out of the bathroom. "Who was that?"

"Your date."

"What did he want?"

"You. He sounded very eager."

"Cora."

"Most men are. Never mind. You get ready for him." Cora headed for the door. "I'll make sure your other man doesn't burn the burgers."

CHAPTER 8

Sherry spotted him the minute she came in the door. He wasn't that hard to spot. An Asian man in the Country Kitchen certainly stood out. He was a handsome man, every hair in place, immaculately dressed, not that old, not that young.

His eyes lit up when he saw her. He got up from his bar stool, walked over and introduced himself.

Sherry, impressed, allowed herself to be led to a table.

He summoned a waitress, ordered her a drink.

He waited until the waitress scurried off, then smiled. "You are as attractive as I hoped you would be."

Flattery made her uncomfortable. Sherry wondered if it was a cultural thing, like being polite. "Forgive me, but have we met?"

"I am sorry to say we have not."

"Then how did you recognize me?"

He smiled. "You are a bright woman. Can you tell me?"

"Is this a test? To see how I might handle a business deal?"

"I am sure you will handle a business deal very well. But we will not talk of it until you have your drink."

"All right. You didn't recognize me. I recognized you. When you *saw* that I had recognized you, you knew who I must be."

"Yes. Of course. I am Japanese. You know it is me. So I know it is you."

The waitress slid drinks in front of them.

He raised his glass. "To the book."

Sherry liked him. He was direct, straight-forward, put her at her ease. Sherry was sure she could deal with him. She smiled as she raised her glass.

From the door to the men's room, Dennis Pride glared daggers at his ex-wife and companion. Dennis had had a few himself, or he might not have violated the restraining order. He had been a good boy lately, but rumors of Sherry's wedding persisted, even if no date was set.

Dennis had snuck off that afternoon to practice with his old band, Tune Freaks, just as his wife, Brenda, suspected him of doing. She was always nagging him about it. As if there was anything wrong with playing music. It wasn't like he was out with another woman. Drinking and laughing in a bar.

Like Sherry and her mystery man. Who the hell was he? It didn't matter. Whoever he was, Sherry shouldn't be out with him.

She'd be sorry.

CHAPTER 9

Sherry was late getting home. She was also a little bit tipsy. Aaron didn't notice, but Cora spirited her into the office on the pretext of needing her help.

Sherry was giggling when Cora put her in the chair. "What can you possibly want to talk about now?"

"Your wedding?"

"What about my wedding?"

"Don't blow it."

"Huh?"

"Sherry, how many drinks did you have?"

"I don't know."

"You don't know?"

"No."

"Did you sign anything?"

"Of course I signed something. That was the whole point."

"You're doing a sudoku book?"

"*You're* doing a sudoku book. I don't do sudoku. You're the sudoku person."

"I solve them. I don't create them."

"Construct."

"Huh?"

"Construct. You don't construct them."

"Right. You're the constructor. I'm the pretty face."

"And I'm the ugly stepsister." Sherry giggled.

"Are you drunk?"

"I can't tell. I've had too much to drink."

"Oh, dear."

"Cora, I'm fine. I signed a book deal. It's not like I haven't done deals with Japan. Different publisher. Same deal. Same advance. Same percent."

"Except I have to write it." Cora took Sherry by the shoulders. "Listen to me. You're engaged to the most calm, broadminded, rational man in the world. You went out for a business meeting and did absolutely nothing wrong. You didn't do anything wrong, did you?"

"Of course not."

"So, you know how a man as understanding as Aaron is going to feel about it?"

"How?"

"Jealous, suspicious, and worried as hell. Men are idiots where women are concerned. If you think Dennis is obsessive, wait'll you give Aaron a few things to think about."

"Oh, come on, Cora. How could Aaron mind? A middle-aged Japanese business-man? I mean, he's very nice, but it was strictly business."

The phone rang. Cora snatched it up.

It was Hideki Takiyama. "Is Miss Sherry Carter there?"

"Sorry. She's not available right now," Cora said, and hung up the phone.

"Who was that?"

"That was your date."

"Why didn't you let me talk to him?"

"Because you're not thinking rationally. If you were, you'd realize you don't want to talk to him."

"You're mean."

"Yeah, I'm just a Grinch."

"And you're jealous."

Cora grimaced. That was at least partly true. "Come on, sober up. I need your help."

"Huh?"

Cora pulled the crossword out of her purse, shoved it in Sherry's face. "Recognize this?"

"Sure. It's one of the Puzzle Lady columns from last week."

"Which one?"

"I don't know. I'd have to solve it."

"Could you do that for me?"

"Why?"

"The schmuck who got killed had it in his pocket."

"A photocopy of a Puzzle Lady puzzle?"

"No. A *newspaper* with a Puzzle Lady puzzle. Harper copied the puzzle so I could solve it."

"Oh, come *on!*"

Cora put up her hands. "What can I tell you? Harper wants me to solve it. *I* know it means nothing. *He* knows it means nothing. He still wants it solved. So I gotta do it. So you gotta do it. So do it."

"Aw, hell. I don't even remember this one."

"You don't have to remember it. You just have to solve it." Cora stuck a pencil in Sherry's hand. "Come on. It'll sober you up."

CHAPTER 10

Cora bought a skim latte and a raisin bran muffin at Cushman's Bakeshop, and carried them down the street to the police station. Chief Harper, who had already finished his muffin, looked enviously at Cora's.

"What kind of muffin is that?"

"Raisin bran."

"I thought you like cranberry scones."

"I do."

"That's not a scone."

"No, it's a muffin. Sherry had one the other day, and it looked good."

"Is it?"

"You want a bite of my muffin?"

Harper sighed. "The last thing I need is to get hooked on another kind of muffin."

"Right. You'd have to start each day making decisions. Horrible for a police chief."

"Give me a bite."

Cora broke off a piece of the muffin, handed it over.

"Damn. It *is* good."

"Yeah. For a woman who can't bake a lick, Mrs. Cushman has mighty good muffins."

"Where's she get her stuff from?"

"Silver Moon. On the Upper West Side. Best bakery in Manhattan."

Harper considered. "You know, I hate to plunge into a murder case on an empty stomach."

"Go on, Chief. I'll hold down the desk until you get back."

Cora sat in Chief Harper's chair, studied the notebook open on his desk.

Walter Krebbs. Thirty-eight years of age. Married. Divorced. No children. Apartment in Washington Heights. Drove a 2000 tan Chevy. License plate: FYI 3205. *FYI* made it a plate Cora could remember.

Time of death was listed as twenty-four to forty-eight hours prior to medical examination. That upped the estimate from the twelve Barney Nathan had originally given.

Cora finished the report and was back in her own chair when Chief Harper came in with his muffin and a steaming Styrofoam cup of black coffee.

"Okay," Harper said. "The world looks a little better now. What can I do for you, Cora?"

"The fellow who got killed."

Harper shrugged. "What about him?"

"What have you got so far?"

"Just what it says in my case notes."

"Huh?"

"I assume you read the file while I got my coffee. That saves me having to tell you about it." Harper gestured to the *Baker-haven Gazette* on his desk. "So you can feed it to Aaron Grant."

Cora frowned. "What do mean, feed it to Aaron Grant? I told you I was checking facts for him. I called you last night to get the name right."

"Oh, he got the name right," Chief Harper said drily. "He also got the fact the victim had a crossword puzzle and a sudoku in his pocket."

"Oh."

"I thought you told me they don't mean anything."

"They don't."

"So why am I reading about them in today's paper?"

"Sorry, Chief. We're a little thin on facts. No murder weapon. No motive. No suspect. Just a corpse. And most likely the guy wasn't even killed here. Aaron's gotta write something."

"So you gave him the puzzles?"

"They don't mean anything. What could

71

it hurt?"

"I don't know. So, did you solve 'em for me?"

"Sure." Cora reached in her drawstring purse, pulled out the photocopy. "Here's the puzzle. Remember? *'The Puzzle Lady has some advice in case an unexpected guest drops in for dinner.'*"

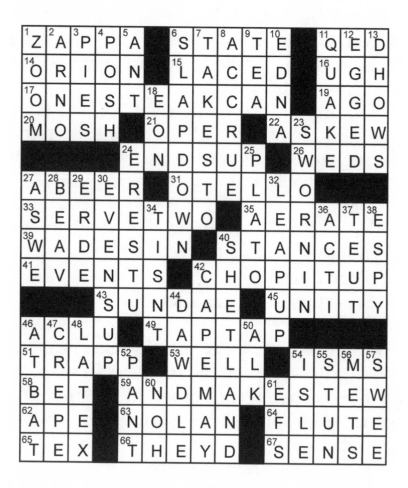

Harper took it, read, " 'One steak can serve two. Chop it up and make stew.' And that's how to deal with an unexpected guest?"

"Yeah. If it sheds any light on your murder, I'll eat it."

"Well, 'chop it up.' The guy did have his head cut open."

"Yeah, because of the puzzle," Cora said, sarcastically. "Good thing it didn't say put the steak in a Cuisinart."

"You have a point." Chief Harper took a bite of muffin. "What about the sudoku?"

"Right here."

Cora passed it over.

Harper frowned. "What the hell does that mean?"

7	2	1	4	8	5	6	3	9
3	4	5	9	6	7	1	8	2
6	9	8	3	1	2	4	7	5
1	8	9	6	3	4	5	2	7
4	3	7	2	5	1	8	9	6
5	6	2	7	9	8	3	4	1
2	1	4	8	7	6	9	5	3
9	7	6	5	4	3	2	1	8
8	5	3	1	2	9	7	6	4

"Absolutely nothing, Chief. You wanted it solved, so I solved it. But it doesn't mean a damn thing."

"I suppose." Harper cocked his head. "About that publisher . . ."

"Oh. You check him out?"

"Yeah. Respectable Japanese businessman. Publishes many American authors. Excellent reputation. Eager to make a name for himself. That's why he'd go out of his way to come here to meet you."

"I see."

"So what's his story? Did you stand the guy up?"

"No. Why?"

"He was in here a half hour ago wanting to know if I'd seen you. Apparently, he'd been asking around, got the impression you hung out here." Harper shrugged. "I can't imagine why. You were supposed to sign something. About doing a book."

"What is he, nuts? Sherry signed it last night."

"But you didn't?"

"I don't have to. She's got my power of attorney. He knew that."

"Well, he must have misunderstood. The guy seemed pretty upset."

The phone rang.

Chief Harper scooped it up. "Bakerhaven

74

police. Harper, here . . . Really . . . What did you find? . . . Can you fax that over? . . . What about his office? . . . Any record of who hired him? . . . Uh-huh. Okay, fax me the records."

He hung up the phone. "New York police. They still haven't found the guy's car. Or any indication where he was killed. Apparently, it wasn't his home or his office."

Cora was looking at him. "What was that you were saying about any record of who hired him?"

"Well, it appears the dead man was a private investigator."

"*Really?* Why wasn't he carrying any identification?"

Chief Harper said nothing.

"Oh. He *was* carrying ID, but you didn't see fit to tell me."

"You didn't ask."

"No, I didn't," Cora said, drily. "If I had, Aaron could have put it in the paper. Instead of that bit about puzzles."

"The guy was a PI. We have no idea who hired him or what he was working on at the time of his death. We'll be going over his records looking for a clue. As soon as we find one, I'll be sure to pass it on."

"That's nice of you, Chief."

"I'm not holding out on you, Cora. It's

just at the moment, I got nothing to go on."

"Are you asking me to solve the case for you, Chief?"

"Absolutely not. And you can quote me on that. It's a police matter, in which you have no business meddling." Chief Harper waggled his finger at her sternly. "And any evidence you may find while not meddling in it, you bring directly to me."

CHAPTER 11

Sherry Carter was getting a jump on the next day's puzzle when a car came up the drive. She frowned. Aaron was back too soon. Another fifteen minutes and she'd have had it knocked. She should call him on his cell phone, send him on an errand to the store.

It occurred to her that was not the type of thing a young woman should do until *after* she was married. When it crossed her mind, she was angry. Why did she have that thought? That was not her thought. That was Cora's thought. That was a cynical old married woman's thought. Not the happy, carefree thought of a young woman in love.

Okay, Sherry realized. Her initial premise was wrong. She should not be irritated that Aaron was back early. She should be delighted. She should meet him at the door. Perhaps in a special garment. Well, let's not go overboard. It was, after all, still mid-morning on a Monday. A cheerful "how do you do" should suffice.

Sherry heard Aaron at the front door. She slapped a smile on her face, skittered down the hall.

Stopped dead.

Dennis Pride stood in the doorway. He'd been drinking. Sherry didn't even have to smell his breath. Not that he was disheveled. He wore a suit and tie, and his hair was combed. But there was something in his manner. He had a look in his eyes. A look she knew well. Back in the days when he was still her husband. When he used to drink.

And hit her.

"What do you think you're doing?" he said.

The words sent a chill down her spine. That was what he used to say years ago. When they were married. Those simple words. That escalated into arguments, no matter how hard she tried to diffuse them. Arguments that led to a slap. Or a punch. Or a kick. Followed by sobbing apologies, pleas for forgiveness, and promises to do better. The nightmare. The never-ending nightmare.

Sherry hesitated, knowing anything she said would be wrong. As would saying nothing. Even a simple, "Hello, Dennis," wouldn't do. In his present state of mind he could twist and turn even the most innocuous remark.

There was no reason for pretense. Sherry's only course of action was the one she wished she had the strength to take throughout her whole rocky marriage. Telling him simply how she felt.

"You shouldn't be here, Dennis."

His lip curled. "Oh, really? You've got a lot of nerve telling me that."

"I've got a restraining order, Dennis."

"Of course you do. You can't trust yourself to tell me to stay away. You know you couldn't do it."

"You're drunk."

"Oh, look who's talking. How's your head feel this morning?"

"I beg your pardon?"

"You didn't get drunk last night? Am I misinformed?"

"Who told you that?"

"So, it's true, is it?"

"I don't know what you're talking about."

"You're lying. Strange. Lying isn't like you. Or is it? All those times you said nothing was going on. Maybe there really was. You just wouldn't admit it."

Sherry's head was coming off. He was

right about her hangover, wrong about everything else. And here he was, back in predivorce mode, jealous, suspicious, paranoid, irrationally accusing her of assignations that had never taken place, indiscretions not committed, whipping himself into a frenzy upon getting no satisfaction, because there could *be* no satisfaction, only a spiraling descent into frustration and abuse.

"Don't touch me Dennis. If you touch me, you know what happens? Brenda dumps you, her father cuts you off, and you go to jail. I swear to God, I'll make it happen."

"Bitch!" Dennis snarled. But he held his ground.

"Here's what we're going to do. You're going to leave, and I'm going to forget you were ever here. I'm not going to report this to the police. I am going to butt out of your life. Just like you are going to butt out of mine."

"What about the paperboy?"

"We're not talking about Aaron."

"No. We're talking about the guy in the bar. Does the paperboy know about the guy in the bar?"

"Drop it, Dennis."

"He looked like a Jap. Is he a Jap?"

Sherry's face froze. "You were there?"

"Ah, now you've changed you tune. Can't

deny it now, can you?

"Dennis, you can't follow me around."

"Hey, if you're going to let yourself get picked up in a bar, and start slugging them back with some Asian playboy —"

"It was a business deal! Didn't you see me sign the paper?" Sherry was furious. Not at Dennis. At herself. For explaining. For answering his charges. As if he had any right to make them. As if she had anything to explain.

Dennis had won and he knew it. His lip curled in triumph, gloating. "So why'd you have another drink? After you signed the paper?"

"You were spying on me?"

"We're talking about you. After you signed the paper, you stayed and had another drink."

"People drink on a deal," Sherry said, and immediately regretted it. Another justification.

"But you *had* a drink," Dennis said. "You signed the paper, you sat there, you finished your drink. Sushi-Boy ordered another."

"Damn it, Dennis!"

A car pulled into the driveway. Sherry had never been so happy to hear the sound of tires on gravel.

"We've got company, Dennis. Who do you

think it is? I bet you ten bucks it's Brenda. When you show up here, she's never far behind. She's very intuitive. Always knows when you start to lose it."

"It better not be."

It wasn't. It was Aaron. He came in, saw Dennis. Stopped. Set his jaw. "All right. You got ten seconds to get out that door, before I carry you out in little pieces."

"You know where she was last night?" Dennis grinned wickedly. "You tell him where you were?"

"I mean it, Dennis."

"She tell you about her little business meeting?"

"One, two . . ."

"You're not really counting to ten, are you? How childish."

". . . three, four . . ."

"She tell you about the drink *after* she signed the contract?"

". . . five, six . . ."

"I mean, why should she get drunk with the guy after the business deal is done?"

". . . seven, eight . . ."

"Fine. I'm going. I'm sure you two have a lot to talk about."

Dennis went out, slamming the door.

Aaron turned to Sherry. "What the hell was *that* all about?"

"He's drunk, Aaron."

"I see that. What's he doing here?"

"Why are you asking me? He gets drunk, he acts out. I have no control over him."

"You call the cops?"

"Not yet."

"What do you mean, not yet?"

"I was afraid he'd get physical. He was right on the edge."

Aaron took a breath. "What was he talking about?"

"What do you mean?"

"About the contract."

"You *know* about the contract."

"About having a drink after the contract?"

"Oh, for Christ's sake!"

"Don't get angry at me. He's the one who brought it up."

"And now *you're* bringing it up."

"Well, what did he mean?"

"He didn't mean anything. He's upset we're getting married. He's trying to break us up."

"How did he know about your business meeting?"

"I guess he was there."

"Last night?"

"Yes."

"Did you see him?"

"No. Of course not."

"Why do you say 'of course not'?"

"If I had, I would have told you."

"Would you have called the police?"

"Huh?"

"Last night. If you'd seen him in the Country Kitchen."

"Aaron, don't do this."

"Do what?"

"Blame me for what I might or might not have done. It is not my hypothetical fault."

"No, of course not. So what's this about an extra drink?"

"What?"

"After you signed the contract, you stayed for —"

"That's it! I've had it! I can only deal with one jealous moron at a time!"

"You're equating me with Dennis?"

"You're equating yourself with Dennis. Don't do it."

"Fine," Aaron said. "I just stopped by to see how you were. I guess I shouldn't have bothered."

Aaron slammed out the door.

Sherry heard his car start.

Oh, hell. What had she done? Was it her throbbing head that made it hard to think, made her mistake which man she blamed for what?

Sherry ran to the door, flung it open.

Aaron was backing down the drive.

She waved, but he didn't see her. Either that or he pretended not to. His head was turned. She couldn't tell.

"Aaron!" Sherry cried.

The car kept going. It reached the bottom of the drive, backed out into the road.

Sherry stumbled down the driveway, waving her arms.

In the house, the phone was ringing, but Sherry couldn't hear.

CHAPTER 12

Sherry's world had shattered. Cora knew it the moment she walked in the door and smelled pancakes. Sherry never ate a hot lunch unless she was upset. She made sandwiches, nibbled on salad greens. Pancakes was comfort food.

Something had gone wrong.

Cora came into the kitchen where Sherry was poking the batter with a spatula. "You make enough for me?"

"You can save me from eating eight."

"You in an eight-pancake funk?"

"Damn near."

"What happened?"

Sherry told Cora about the dustup between Aaron and Dennis.

Cora sat at the kitchen table, pulled out her smokes.

"Not while I'm cooking," Sherry said.

"Ah, hell," Cora said. "How do you expect me to play therapist if I can't smoke?"

"I don't expect you to play therapist."

"Well, someone better. You're not doing yourself any good."

"Do you blame me?"

"No. You're a victim of circumstance. Now, circumstance is over. Time to climb out of it."

"Like it was that easy."

"Fine. *Don't* climb out of it. Just get happy enough to share some pancakes. You got any syrup?"

"In the cupboard."

Cora took out the maple syrup, came back and put it on her pancakes. "Okay, I heard about your troubles, let me tell you mine. The dead guy they found yesterday is a private eye from New York. The clues are all in the city so I can't follow 'em."

Cora brought Sherry up to date on the investigation.

"I guess we're both a little down on our luck," Sherry said.

"Yeah. And why do you keep avoiding the Japanese guy? He's trying to get in touch with you."

"Why? I signed the contract."

"I don't know. The guy seems to feel the deal isn't finalized. You sure it was a contract, not a letter of intent?"

"It doesn't matter. Either one would seal

the deal."

"Well, will you call him and tell him so he'll stop bugging me? He acts like you're ducking him."

"Oh?"

Cora's eyes widened. "Of course. You *are* ducking him. Dennis thinks you got too cozy with the guy. Just because he's Dennis doesn't make him wrong. You came home drunk last night. Dennis got Aaron all worked up about it. Instead of telling Aaron Dennis is all wet, you're sulking and eating pancakes. Why? Because you feel guilty. For going out drinking with a dashing young rogue with bedroom eyes and a scar on his chin."

"Scar?"

"Amazing how it adds to his mystique. I can think of a lot of men I'd have married if they just had a scar."

"He doesn't have a scar, Cora."

"Don't be silly. Hideki has a scar on his chin."

"Hideki?"

"Yeah."

"That's not his name."

"Yes, it is."

"Cora, you're terrible with names."

"Not that one. It's the same as Hideki Matsui, the star Yankee outfielder."

"His name's not Hideki, Cora."

"Oh, my God! Where's the contract?"

"In the office."

"Get it."

Sherry took one look at Cora's face, and headed for the door. She was back in moments with the contract.

Cora snatched it from her. "Well, no wonder Hideki's so frantic to see you. You signed a contract with Aoki Yoshiaki!"

Sherry was beside herself. "How could this have happened?"

"I have no idea."

"I wasn't that drunk."

"I'm not saying you were that drunk."

"Well, I wasn't."

Cora shook her head. "This is a politically incorrect nightmare. We've mistaken one Japanese man for another. Like all Japanese men look alike. Japan will stop importing my cereal."

"They import your cereal?"

"How the hell should I know? How could you make this mistake?"

"It was easy. You told me I'd be getting a call from a Japanese publisher. I *got* a call from a Japanese publisher. I can't help it if it was the *wrong* Japanese publisher."

"We've gotta break the contract," Cora said. "Can we do that?"

"I don't know. Under what grounds can you break a contract?"

"If it was entered into under duress."

"That would be hard to prove."

"Or deception."

"There you go."

Cora grimaced. "The guy called you up, asked you out to discuss a contract, bought you a drink, showed you a contract, which you signed. The only thing he did deceptive was look Japanese, which I do not believe is legal grounds for breaking a contract."

"Shall we call Becky Baldwin?"

"Yeah, right," Cora said. "Now your ex-husband's stuck his nose in, let's throw Aaron's ex-girlfriend in for good measure."

"So what are we going to do?"

"We're going to sit down with Hideki, and we're going to be very contrite, and we're going to apologize, and we're going to see if there's any way out. He's a publisher, surely this has happened to him before."

"You mean we'll ask him what to do?"

"Exactly."

"Fine. We'll do that."

"Just one thing."

"What's that?"

"You know how bad I am at faces." Cora grimaced. "Scar or no scar, if I start to

introduce you to the wrong Japanese publisher, kick me in the shin."

CHAPTER 13

Hideki Takiyama was nowhere to be found. At least, he wasn't at any of the obvious places. He wasn't at the Country Kitchen, he wasn't in the Wicker Basket, he wasn't hanging out at Cushman's Bakeshop. If he was at the shopping mall the odds of finding him weren't that great, since they didn't know what his car looked like. They drove out anyway, checked the Starbucks, and cruised the parking lot scanning the stores to no avail.

"Why don't you have his phone number?" Sherry griped.

"You weren't calling him, he was calling you."

"Which was pretty stupid."

"What's stupid about it?"

"That's where it all went wrong. If *I* was calling *him*, I'd *get* him. If he's calling me, how do I know who I'm speaking to?"

"Oh," Cora said defensively. "So now I'm

supposed to have *anticipated* a second Japanese publisher trying to ace the other Japanese publisher out?"

"Well, you should have given me his name."

"I didn't remember his name."

"Oh? I thought it was some Yankee pitcher you couldn't forget."

"Yankee outfielder."

"Exactly. So how could you forget?"

"I didn't forget. I just didn't think it was important."

"You said you forgot."

"It's a figure of speech."

"It's *not* a figure of speech. It's a *lie.*"

"Well, a lie is a figure of speech."

"Cora —"

"You must be really upset to try to hold me to what I said."

"I *am* really upset. It doesn't help when your statements are all over the map."

"You'd have made a good lawyer, you know it?"

"Are you comparing me with Becky Baldwin?"

"No, but I can see where your head's at. Look, you and Aaron had a fight. That's normal. Aaron has an ex-girlfriend. That's normal. He's not off boffin' her in the back of his Honda Civic."

Sherry's mouth fell open. "I never thought he was!" she said angrily.

"Atta girl!" Cora said. "That's what I want to hear. Now, take that positive attitude and build on it."

"Damn it, Cora —"

"Uh-uh." Cora waggled her finger. "Positive. Positive. Your love life is fine. We've just hit a small business snafu."

"Yeah. Because you couldn't be bothered to get his phone number."

Cora snapped her fingers. "I *did* get his phone number. He gave me his card."

"Where is it?"

"I gave it to Chief Harper."

"You what?"

"To trace the guy. To see if he was someone we should be doing business with. Turns out he is."

"Gee," Sherry said. "Too bad we're not."

"No problem. We'll go get the card from the chief."

Still bickering, Cora and Sherry drove into town, parked in front of the police station.

"You coming in?" Cora said as Sherry got out of the car.

"Yes, I'm coming in."

"Then try not to act like I drowned your puppy."

"Are you telling me not to be a bitch?"

"I thought I phrased it better. But you're the linguist."

Dan Finley was manning the desk.

"Harper here?" Cora asked the young officer.

Dan shook his head. "Got a robbery. I wanted to go, but the chief took it himself. I think he's bored. But you didn't hear it from me."

"What got robbed?"

"Antique shop."

"Wilber's?"

"No. Meachem's. Out on Oak Lane. You know it?"

"They all sort of blend together." Cora hadn't been antiquing since her third husband, Frank, dragged her all over creation looking for Queen Anne chairs. She'd divorced him shortly thereafter. "Chief been out there long?"

"He just left. Something I can help you with?"

"Need to see him. We'll take a run out."

"You know where it is?"

"Past the old mill?"

"That's it."

"We could have called," Sherry said, as they drove out of town.

"Huh?"

95

"We could have called him from the station."

"I hate to call a guy at a crime scene. That's rude."

"But it's okay to barge in on him?"

"We're not barging. We're dropping by."

"Yeah, sure. You just want to see the crime scene."

"Don't you?"

"An antique-store robbery?" Sherry said. "Not likely."

"What's the matter? You afraid Aaron may be covering it?"

"I never thought any such thing."

"Well, you should have. If you want to be manipulative and controlling, you got to stay on top of your game."

"Cora —"

"Take it from a pro."

"Keep your hands on the wheel."

The antique shop was white with black shutters, which differed from the other antique shops in town in no way whatsoever, which was one of the reasons Cora had trouble telling them apart. The sign, MEACHEM'S ANTIQUES, hanging from wooden posts, was discreetly tucked back from the sidewalk so as not to offend the eye. Or attract it. The sign blended in with the building, and hugged the ground. In deep snow it probably couldn't be seen at all.

Chief Harper's patrol car was parked out front. There was no sign of the chief, and the door of the shop was closed. Cora tried it, found it locked.

"Hmm. After the horse was out," she muttered.

"Huh?" Sherry said.

"Come on."

Cora led the way around the building, was immediately rewarded by the sight of a broken window.

"Chief! You in there?" Cora called.

There came the sound of stomping, then Chief Harper stuck his head through the glass.

"Hey, don't cut yourself, Chief. What's going on here?"

"Funny you should ask."

"Oh?"

"You found me, so you must have stopped by the station. If you did that, Dan Finley must have told you I was out at a robbery. You're looking through a broken window. I gotta figure you're pretty much up to date."

"Are you saying that I know as much as you do?"

His face might have reddened. With him bent over, peering out the window it was hard to tell. "I'll be right there."

Cora and Sherry went around to the front of the house in time to meet Chief Harper and a man, presumably Mr. Meachem, coming out the door. Cora had seen the antiquer around town. It was hard not to. The man was plump, gave the impression the antique business was good.

Except today.

"Cora. Sherry. You know Mr. Meachem."

"Guess you had a little break-in," Cora said.

"A little break-in? That's one way to put it. They smashed my window with a rock."

"You didn't hear it?"

"I wasn't here."

"When did it happen?"

"Last night. I was at the movies."

"You discovered it when you got home?"

"No, not till today. But I didn't hear it. And I'm a light sleeper."

Cora doubted that. "So you found it this morning?"

"This afternoon. First time I went in the room."

"Anything missing?"

"I haven't taken inventory."

"But anything you noticed?"

Chief Harper elbowed his way in. "Actually, *I* was asking the questions. Some of these we've already covered."

"It never hurts to go over it again," Cora said. "You'd be surprised what people remember the second time around."

Meachem smiled. "Not this time. We've been over the same ground twice."

"Did you check the display windows?"

Chief Harper frowned.

Meachem said irritably, "Didn't you hear? The display windows weren't broken. It was the room over there. I've been going through it, but so far nothing's missing."

"I wouldn't expect anything would be," Cora said. "The crook didn't break in to steal anything in the side room. He doesn't *know* what's in the side room. He sees something he wants in the display window. He doesn't want to break a huge sheet of plate glass, so he breaks a small window on the side. That's what I'd do if I were robbing the place. Not that I would. But if did, I'd make a good job of it."

"Well, is there anything missing from the display windows?" Chief Harper said.

"Absolutely not. The gold necklace is there. The Venetian glass vase. The buffalo nickel collection. Not that it's for sale, they're just samples of what I have on hand. The Confederate army cap. You don't see that in many Yankee shops. How could a robber not take that?"

"How, indeed?" Cora said.

"And the silver tea set. And the ruby earrings. And the —"

He broke off, gawking.

"What is it?" Chief Harper said.

"The sword! I had it for years, nobody gave a damn. The price nearly tripled since the movie."

"What movie?"

"The Quentin Tarantino thing. With Uma Thurman and Daryl Hannah. And David Carradine."

"*Kill Bill*?" Cora said.

"That's right."

Cora's eyes widened. "You mean . . . ?"

"That's right. Just like in the movie. A priceless, handcrafted, samurai sword."

CHAPTER 14

"This is very bad," Chief Harper said.

They were back in the police station. Chief Harper had dispatched Dan Finley to put out an APB on the missing sword. What exactly that entailed, Cora had no idea, but it sounded impressive, even if it only meant putting up a flier in the post office.

"Bad enough someone's got to steal a samurai sword, but they would have to do it when a Japanese businessman's in town."

"You don't know the half of it," Cora said.

"Huh?"

Cora filled Chief Harper in on the Japanese situation.

Harper was puzzled. "I traced one publisher for you, so you signed with another?"

"Sherry had too much to drink," Cora explained.

Sherry's mouth fell open. Before she could bite her aunt's head off, Cora said, "Relax. If I can't drink, at least I can rag the people who do. The point is, there's two Japanese businessmen running around town who don't seem to like each other."

"You think they're competitive enough one of them might want to stab the other with a sword?"

"Publishing's getting more and more cut-throat," Cora said. "I blame Barnes and Noble and Amazon.com."

Chief Harper squinted at her. "You're kidding."

"Glad you noticed. Much as I like the idea of men killing themselves over me, I can't see them killing themselves over my book."

"Nonetheless, we have a sword missing."

"Yes, we do. Coincidentally, we happen to have a corpse with half a face."

"But . . ."

"But what?"

"That was before the robbery."

"Says who?"

"Mr. Meachem."

"Yeah," Cora said. "And he's basing that on the fact he went to the movies, so that's when he figures the robber broke in. But what if it happened the day before? He just didn't have reason to go in that room, so he didn't see the broken glass."

"But he'd notice the sword was missing."

"No, he wouldn't. The guy must have

walked past the window half a dozen times. Until he started listing what was in it, he didn't know what was gone."

Chief Harper snatched up the phone, punched in a number. "It's Harper. Let me talk to him . . . Barney? . . . I got a question about the dead man . . . No, I haven't solved it yet, thank you very much . . . Yes, I know I'm always hounding you for the medical report, it's not quite the same thing. Can I ask you a question without you telling every patient who comes in? . . . Fine, we're even. Here's the thing. The dead man with half a face. Could the part that's missing have been carved away with a samurai sword? . . . No, I haven't been drinking. Could a sword inflict a wound like that. Say it was very sharp. Like a Ginsu knife, that slices and dices . . . It's hardly a laughing matter, Barney."

Harper slammed down the phone. "Son of a bitch! Oh, beg your pardon, Cora."

"From the extent of Barney's ridicule, I take it he doesn't think much of that notion."

"It's a tough concept to sell. Anyway, he can't see a sword being sharp enough to inflict such a wound."

"Guess he didn't see Uma Thurman cut the top of Lucy Liu's head off."

"That's a movie. Unless it was some special whoop-de-do sword worth a small fortune . . ."

"A million bucks. I suppose Mr. Meachem isn't claiming that?"

"Six hundred fifty. That's probably inflated for his insurance claim. It's not apt to be that sharp."

"Even so. With a weapon like that stolen, you kind of like to see it used in a murder."

"Cora."

"Well, you do. The guy's dead anyway. He won't be any less dead if the circumstances are bizarre."

"I hate to rain on your parade, but the guy was hit with something more substantial, like an ax."

"How can you tell?"

"The murder weapon wasn't thin or razor-blade sharp. I'll tell you what Barney just told me. You cut a cantaloupe in half, the knife goes through, makes a perfect cut. You hit a cantaloupe with an ax, not so pretty. You saw the corpse. It was not so pretty."

"Cantaloupes don't bleed."

"So, Barney says it wasn't a sword. You got a problem with that, take it up with him."

"I'll do that. Meanwhile, you got a line on anyone might be interested in a samurai sword?"

"Such as?"

"Well, you got two Japanese men running around town."

"Are you suggesting I resort to racial profiling?"

"Heaven forbid. Still, you might expect a publisher to be knowledgeable, and solicit his advice."

"Isn't that the equivalent of the British police having someone 'assist them with their enquiries'?"

"I'm not suggesting you put anyone in custody."

"Well, what are you suggesting I do?"

"Find them."

CHAPTER 15

Cora and Sherry came out of the police station and met Aaron Grant on his way in.

"Aaron!" Sherry said. "Where are you going?"

"I'm going to report a crime."

"What?"

"Evidently Dennis took exception to my car being parked in front of Sherry's house. He smashed my headlight."

"You're kidding!" Cora said.

Aaron pointed. "See for yourself."

"How come you're just reporting it now?"

"I didn't see it."

"Oh?"

Aaron made a face. "All right, maybe he didn't smash it then. Maybe he saw it parked in front of the paper."

"How do you know it was him?"

"Exactly," Sherry said. "You're a newsman. You ought to know the difference between 'knowing' something and being able to prove it.”

“Yeah, we say *alleged.* Look, Sherry, my car was vandalized. It doesn't matter who did it, it's still a crime.”

“Are you going to say Dennis did it?”

“You mean will I allege it?”

Cora put up her hands. “Kids. This is beneath you. A moron who breaks people's headlights does not deserve to get his way by causing friction between you. Do you need me to referee?”

Sherry suggested a more stimulating solitary entertainment.

“Nice talk,” Cora said. “Do you suppose you could modulate your tone? We're about to have company.”

Sherry looked around to find a well-dressed Japanese businessman bearing down on them. He was a handsome young man, with a devil-may-care, cocky attitude, and a scar on his chin.

He strode right by her up to Cora. “Ms. Felton. I have been looking for you. I am still not able to contact your niece.”

“It's not as hard as you think. That's her right there. Hideki Takiyama, this is Sherry Carter, and her fiancé, Aaron Grant.”

Hideki's face broke into an enormous smile. “I am very pleased to meet you. It has been, how do you say, a frustration.

Cora says you are the one to whom I must speak business. Has she told you about me?"

"Of course."

"Perhaps we could all have lunch and on conclusion discuss the matter then."

Sherry sighed. "Mr. Takiyama —"

"Hideki."

"We have a little problem."

"Oh?"

"It's somewhat embarrassing."

"I don't understand."

"Oh, tell him, for goodness sakes," Cora said. "Some other guy aced you out."

Hideki frowned. "Aced me out?"

"Tricked you. Scammed you. Pulled a fast one. On you, and on us, too."

"What do you mean?"

"Someone called my niece and pretended to be you."

"Pretended to be me?"

"Not you. He pretended *he* was the publisher she was told would be calling."

Hideki's eyes blazed. "Aoki Yoshiaki!"

"Can I help you?"

All heads turned to the dapper, young Japanese man who had just come out of Cushman's Bakeshop with a cappuccino.

Sherry immediately recognized her drinking companion. His smile, which had seemed suave and charismatic, was arrogant and mocking now.

"Ah, Hideki. How nice to see you. You were talking with my author?"

It occurred to Cora that Hideki resembled nothing so much as a cartoon character with steam coming out of his ears. She would not have been surprised to see him explode.

Hideki stepped out in the street to meet the other man. They approached each other like Western gunfighters, then circled like alpha male dogs about to battle over a bitch in heat.

Cora panicked. What if she couldn't tell them apart? Of course, she could. Though similarly dressed, their features were different. She could pick out Hideki anywhere. Even without the scar.

"You came here to steal my writer," Hideki charged.

"You came here to steal mine."

"Which you stole from me."

"You talk of stealing. I talk of friendly competition."

"Friendly?"

"Yes. May the best man win."

Hideki scowled. "Always the English idioms."

"You do not like how I talk?" Aoki smiled. "Who is the American?"

"You lived here."

"I was not born here. I am Japanese."

"You are a thief!"

"You dare to call me that!"

Cora Felton was torn between going into the police station for help, and pulling her gun. It was a toss-up. Brandishing a weapon was much more fun. But holding your new publisher at gunpoint was probably not a course of action many literary agents would be apt to endorse.

"What are you doing!?"

The high-pitched voice froze the two combatants.

A geisha girl came striding across the street. She was stunning, in yards of brightly colored silk, pale makeup, and sculptured black hair. In her Japanese garb she was gorgeous, but at the moment she had a most disapproving look on her face, like a mother about to lecture a naughty child.

She strode up to the two men, heaved a huge breath, let it out like a fire-breathing dragon, and launched into a tirade of the most staccato Japanese Cora had ever heard outside of a nail salon.

The effect was dazzling. Both men wilted like steamed spinach. Every bit of macho posturing vanished instantly. What could only be sputtered apologies were cut short as the woman, brooking no nonsense, dismissed Aoki with a wave of her hand, and watched imperiously as he slunk off in the direction from which he'd come, then wheeled on Hideki, spewing an unbroken stream of invective.

When the woman had bitch-slapped the poor man silly, she stretched out her arm, pointed in the opposite direction from which Aoki had gone.

Docilely, and without a word, Hideki walked away

The woman watched him go, then turned to the others. "I humbly beg your pardon. My husband is a fool. His friend is an idiot."

"His friend?" Cora said.

She waved her hand. "They fight. But they are old friends. They just want to win."

"You mean like the contract?" Sherry said.

The woman sized her up. "You are the one who signed the contract?"

"Yes. I'm Sherry Carter."

"I am Reiko." She nodded, briefly. "I must apologize for this unfortunate misunderstanding. But it is not your problem. They will work it out."

She curtsied, crossed the street, and went up the steps of the town library.

"Who's that?" Aaron said.

"That's Hideki's wife," Cora said. "Didn't you see how she talked to him."

"Oh, you can tell they're married by the way the wife abuses the husband?" Aaron said.

"Thanks a bunch, Cora," Sherry said dryly.

Cora shrugged. "Hey, I'm happily divorced. Don't let me rain on your parade. Now, before this kabuki group did its little neo–Noh drama, Aaron was headed for the police station. I'm not sure it's necessary or even desirable, but if you insist on reporting an act of vandalism, I would strongly urge that no husbands, living or dead, need be suggested as the proximate cause. The simple report in itself will raise the wariness of the local constabulary, such that the presence of any unlawful, unwelcome, or unauthorized individual will be thoroughly discouraged."

Sherry's mouth was open. "Watch your language, Cora. You're starting to sound like me."

CHAPTER 16

Cora flung herself into a chair in front of Chief Harper's desk, and declared, "I've been here too long!"

The chief looked up in surprise. "You just got here."

"I mean in Bakerhaven. In Connecticut. In this hellhole that passes for a town."

"Hey! That's my hellhole you're talking about."

"I'm a New York girl, born and bred. Proud of it. And everything about it. Well, maybe not the Knicks. But I believe in my inalienable right to cuss out a cabdriver who cuts me off. You know what I mean?"

"I don't even know what you're talking about. You want to go out and come in again, I'll pretend this never happened?"

"I feel old. Addled. Like I've fallen down in the muck and mire and stagnated."

"Does this have anything remotely to do with a police matter?"

"I went to New York last night to check out the dead guy's office."

"You broke into his office?"

"That's not the type of question you want to ask me. Because, if I had, and I told you, you'd have to turn me in. Or you'd be guilty of suppressing evidence. Be a hell of a mess. Luckily, I didn't, so you're in the clear. But just for future reference."

"What *did* you do?"

Cora grimaced. "Not a great question, either. Of course, it's easier to evade, fabricate, and/or lie about."

"Why are you giving me a hard time?"

"I'm frustrated, and I'm taking it out on you. Anyway, here's the deal. I figure since the police had no luck with Walter Krebb's phone records, maybe whoever hired him was a walk-in off the street."

"Wait a minute. How do you know they had no luck with his phone records?"

"If they had they'd have told you. And you'd have told me."

"You're not officially part of this investigation."

"Still, you would and you didn't. So I drove into Manhattan to check his office. It's a second-floor walk-up on Broadway. As luck would have it, there's a newsstand right out front, so I buy a *Daily News,* a fifty-cent investment to ingratiate myself. If I had a client, I'd put it on my expense account. I chat the guy up, bring the conversation back to last week, ask him if he happened to see an Asian guy go in. He just stares at me like I'm some hick from the sticks, which is what I felt like. Then he laughed in my face."

"That's rather rude."

"We were in front of a sushi bar."

Chief Harper suppressed a grin, which made it worse.

"Oh, go on, laugh at me," Cora said. "The fact is, I used to think like a New Yorker, and now I don't think at all."

"Like the rest of us yokels?"

"No offense meant, but it's pretty damn embarrassing."

"Yeah," Harper said. "Why were you looking for an Asian man to begin with?"

"Are you kidding me? Two Japanese publishers hate each other. What's more natural than one would hire a PI to keep tabs on the other?"

"Nothing. Except for the murder. Is it your contention this guy got killed over a bunch of puzzle books? Or do you just like the idea of people fighting over you?"

"I have no idea why the guy got killed. For all I know, the reason he got killed may have nothing to do with the reason he was hired. But something has to make sense. I gotta play the cards I'm dealt."

"So, what's your theory now?"

Cora waggled her hand. "It's not quite formulated."

"No kidding. How much did they pay you for this book?"

"Not that much."

"How much is not that much?"

"I'd have to look at the contract."

"Oh?"

"It's a Japanese contract. Sherry signed it. I don't know if it's in dollars, or euros, or yen. I trust her implicitly, and I'm sure we got a good deal."

"You don't know how much you're making?"

"Sue me. I'm bad at business matters. What's your point?"

"My point is, how is this worth hiring a PI? Doesn't the cost outweigh the benefits? I mean, I'm assuming if you signed a six-figure deal you'd know about it."

"You got that right."

"So how does that make sense?"

"I don't know. But a samurai sword is missing, and there's Japanese men in town." Cora put up her hands. "Not that I'm pointing any fingers."

Harper frowned.

116

"You made any progress on the sword?" Cora said. "You ask the neighbors if they'd seen any Asians skulking around."

"Cora, you can't say that!"

"Why not?"

"It's prejudiced, politically incorrect, and sounds awful."

"Why? If we were looking for a blond, teenage girl, would it be wrong to ask the neighbors if they'd seen any blond, teenage girls skulking around?"

"We don't know we're looking for an Asian. You just think that because of the samurai sword."

"Okay. The stolen goods is the star quarterback's high school letter sweater. Can we ask about blond, teenage girls?"

"I'm not sure you could get away with *blond*."

"You know, Chief, you're going to great lengths not to answer the question."

"What question?"

"Did any of the neighbors see someone skulking around the antique shop?"

"People don't like to tell a policeman they saw someone skulking. It brings up why didn't they report it at the time."

"What's the bottom line, Chief?"

Harper sighed. "No one saw any Asians."

"You *asked* them?"

"Don't quote me."

"You gave me all that trouble and then I find you asked them?"

"I didn't phrase it as bluntly as you did."

"You mean you didn't use the word *skulking?*"

"I don't believe I did."

"So no one saw any Asians. Did anyone see anyone else?"

"Mrs. Clemson, across the street, thought she heard tires screech. Maybe ten-thirty at night. You have to take what she says with a grain of salt. She's a widow, and she's jumpy."

"And you call me politically incorrect?"

"Hey. She's a widow. And she's jumpy. I'm not saying it's cause and effect."

"What's cause and effect?"

"That she's jumpy because she's a widow."

"Really?" Cora smiled sweetly. "What did the woman say?"

"She thought she heard a squeal of brakes. Like a car stopped short. But she was in bed watching TV. By the time she got up and went to the window, the only car in sight was parked across the street."

"In front of the antique shop?"

"No, the next house down. But she thought she saw a drunk walking along the sidewalk."

"A drunk?"

"That was her impression. She didn't stay to watch. She made sure her front door was locked and went back to bed."

"So," Cora said, "you figure if someone drove by the antique shop, saw a sword in the window they wanted to steal, slammed on the brakes, parked the car, and went back to check it out, that could be the drunk the widow saw that night. Any chance the drunk was Asian?"

"Perfectly good chance. There's also a perfectly good chance he was sober. And a perfectly good chance he had nothing to do with the car *or* the antique shop."

"I don't suppose you got a description of the car?"

"That would be a correct assumption. Of course, this all took place after the murder, so it doesn't really matter."

"You're right," Cora said, judiciously. "It certainly doesn't."

CHAPTER 17

Mrs. Clemson wasn't old for a widow. At least in Cora's humble opinion. Cora'd never been a widow, always choosing to divest herself of her husbands while they were still alive. "Better an alimony in the hand than an inheritance in the bush" was Cora's motto. And while there were some husbands she would have liked to kill, there were none she was willing to wait for to die.

"A shame," Cora said. "He sounds like a lovely man."

"He was," Mrs. Clemson said. "And what a good provider. At the office every day, working longer and longer hours."

"What did he do?"

"He was an office manager. For a Manhattan textile firm."

"You say he worked hard?"

"Oh, yes. Even after he fell sick."

"What did he have?"

"Respiratory arrest."

"How old was he?"

"Thirty-nine. Can you believe it? Just thirty-nine."

Cora *could* believe it. A thirty-nine-year-old office manager who spent more and more time in the city, and who undoubtedly had a young secretary, was well within the scheme of her matrimonial expertise, and a prime candidate for domestic surveillance, and a messy but profitable divorce. The death of such a spouse was, in Cora's humble opinion, serendipitous, if not opportunistic. Respiratory arrest, indeed! Her tea, which moments ago had tasted delicious, Cora eyed with suspicion.

"Okay," Cora said. "Let me walk you through this. You're in bed. You hear the squeal of tires. You brace yourself for the crash."

"What crash?"

"I know. There *was* no crash. But don't you always brace yourself?"

"I suppose."

"So you brace yourself for the crash. Which doesn't come. That's odd. You're expecting a crash but you don't get one. Why not? First thought, something in the road, driver swerved to miss it."

"Yes," Mrs. Clemson said. "That's what I thought. Someone ran out in the road."

"Who?"

"What?"

"Who would run out in the road? Are there children on the street?"

"Not that time of night. The Crowleys have a dog. They're not careful. Let it out alone."

Cora didn't care about the Crowleys' dog. Also, she sometimes let Buddy out alone, and didn't like the implied reprimand. "When you got to the window you didn't see anything?"

"No. Not even the car."

"Except the one that was parked."

"Yes."

"What kind was it?"

"I really didn't notice."

Cora nodded. "So, it wasn't a Volkswagen Beetle."

"Why do you say that?"

"Well, that's the type of car you'd notice. Distinctive shape, no way you could miss it."

"That's right."

"And it couldn't have been a sports car, either. You'd have noticed that."

"I guess I would."

"So we're talking some sort of sedan. Not a Hummer, or an SUV. Not anything you'd be sure to notice. Just a nondescript, run-of-the-mill, everyday car."

"Uh-huh."

"And the Japanese man you saw staggering up the street . . . ?"

She frowned. "Wait a minute. Wait a minute. Who said he was Japanese?"

"You didn't say he was Japanese?"

"No."

"I thought you said he was Japanese."

"I didn't say he was Japanese. *You* said he was Japanese."

"So, you're saying he wasn't."

"No, of course not."

"How do you know?"

"I'd have noticed. Just the way I'd have noticed if the car was a VW."

"Very good," Cora said. That was the analogy she was going for. Nice of the woman to make the leap for her. "And this was a man, not a woman?"

"Yes."

"And you think he was drunk?"

"He staggered once. Righted himself, kept going down the street."

"So you kept watching him?"

"No, I went back to bed."

"With a drunk in the street?"

"He wasn't coming my way. Still, I made sure the door was locked."

"And the only thing you remember about

him was he wasn't Japanese?"

"I didn't say that. That's not the only thing I remember."

"Oh?"

"He was well-dressed for a drunk. Not like a town rowdy. He wasn't wearing a coat, just a suit jacket."

"Anything else you can remember?"

Mrs. Clemson thought a moment.

"He had long hair."

CHAPTER 18

Brenda Wallenstein's loft in Soho had been a graduation gift from her father. The spacious, open, floor-through had been the perfect thing for a young woman of artistic aspirations, who could afford not to work. Upon her marriage to Dennis Pride, a number of renovations had been rushed through. The bathtub in the kitchen, for instance, such a source of merriment in wilder days, proved inefficient for a young husband dressing for business. A bath with shower stall had been partitioned off. Brenda's art studio, which had once encompassed the entire floor, was now confined to the front third of the loft, with the remainder divided into living, dining, and bedroom spaces. Bohemian touches still remained in such furnishings as the futon, the macramé wall hangings, the cinder-block bookcase, but the general effect was upscale.

Cora Felton, who had been there once

long ago to pick up Sherry Carter, was impressed. "My, Brenda, you've done marvels with the place."

Brenda eyed Cora suspiciously. "Why are you here?"

"Not the most cordial of greetings, Brenda, considering we have mutual interests."

"Such as?"

"Keeping your husband away from my niece."

Brenda put her hands on her hips defiantly. Her curves bounced loosely beneath a painter's smock. Brenda could have passed for a Rubens model. Zaftig, or what the college boys called pleasingly plump. There was a smudge of oil paint on her left cheek. Some garish shade of orange. Cora shuddered to think what the woman was painting.

"What has Dennis done now?" Brenda demanded.

"Nothing."

"That's right, nothing. Because, if he had, I would have heard. From his attorney, Becky Baldwin, who is not apt to let anything be put over on her."

Cora shook her head. "You're pretty naive, aren't you?"

"What do you mean?"

"My niece is going to marry Aaron Grant. Becky used to be Aaron's girlfriend. If Becky still has feelings for him, she would have a vested interest in seeing the marriage didn't take place. The best way to sabotage the relationship would be to turn a blind eye to Dennis."

"Are you saying she's doing that?"

"Not at all. But it's the sort of thing a scheming, unscrupulous woman would be apt to think of." Cora pursed her lips. "I don't know why I thought of it."

"Could it be because you've busted up more marriages than Angelina Jolie, Cora?"

"Give me a break. She only broke up one. Granted she gets more ink, but, trust me, I'm way ahead."

"Come on, Cora. This isn't like you. Has Dennis done something or not?"

"I don't know. But he's got long hair."

"What?"

"He's grown his hair, hasn't he? He combs it back, he plasters it down. He tucks it under his collar. But all the same, it's really long. If he were drunk, it would flop around. He'd look like he did in his Tune Freaks days."

"You think he's back with the band?"

"Do you?"

"What makes you think he's back with the band?"

"I don't. I'm bluffing. I haven't seen him. I was guessing about his hair being long. Evidently it was a good guess. If it was short, you'd have asked me to leave. So I can assume it isn't. I'm not shocking you, I'm confirming your worst fears. What makes *you* think he's back with the band? Aside from the fact he's growing his hair."

Brenda sighed. Her body rippled underneath the smock. She flopped down on the futon, rubbed her head. "I get phone calls. I answer, they hang up. You know, like, 'if my wife answers, hang up.' Only it's not a girlfriend. I hear talking in the background. Once I heard a drum. Then you come and ask me if he's back in the band."

"Actually, I have no evidence that he is. I just wanted to find out if he'd grown his hair."

"Why?"

"Was Dennis home Sunday night around ten-thirty?"

"Oh, my God! What has he done?"

"You mean he wasn't here?"

"I don't know. I have to think."

"Two nights ago. Ten-thirty. Where were you?"

"Damn!"

"What?"

"He came in drunk."

"What time?"

"I don't know."

"You don't know?"

"Are you going to repeat everything I say?"

"Not if you say something that makes sense."

"I fell asleep watching TV."

"What show?"

"I don't remember. What does it matter?"

"It would help fix the time. You weren't concerned when he didn't come home?"

"I figured he was with the band."

"You said he came home drunk."

"I woke up, he was in the shower. He had an early appointment."

"So?"

"He had hangover breath."

Cora knew it well. "Did he make his appointment?"

"No one complained."

"Are you sure?"

"If they had, I'd have known."

"How?"

"Daddy'd have called me. He keeps his son-in-law on a very short leash."

"Not short enough," Cora muttered.

"What did Dennis do?"

"He might have broken into an antique store."

"You're kidding!"

"No, but I'm going on the flimsiest of evidence."

"What's that?"

"He has long hair."

"Are you nuts?"

"And he was drunk."

"That's ridiculous."

"Yes, it is. Which is why I'm being very careful to tell you I'm not making any accusations."

"But you think he broke into an antique shop?"

"He may have."

"Was anything taken?"

"Yes."

"What?"

"A samurai sword."

Brenda gawked at her. "Why in the world would Dennis steal a samurai sword?"

"I don't know," Cora said. "But I intend to find out."

CHAPTER 19

Aaron looked guilty. Sherry might not have noticed, but Cora did. Cora was an expert on guilty. She could tell just by the way a husband came in the door whether he'd been out on business or pleasure. By the time she married Melvin, Cora had a divorce lawyer on speed dial.

Sherry and Cora were on the couch watching TV when Aaron got home.

"We ate," Sherry said. "Dinner's on the stove."

"I got tied up at work."

"Uh-huh."

"Had a column to finish. Then they threw a rewrite at me."

"If it's cold, you can zap it in the microwave."

"Yeah. Sorry I'm late."

Aaron waited for a reaction. Getting none, he went on into the kitchen.

Cora watched him go. She sighed, shook

her head, heaved herself off the couch. "Need a smoke," she muttered.

Aaron was loading up a plate with lamb shank and risotto.

"Sherry's some cook," Cora said. "That lamb shank falls off the bone. At least it did. It's probably congealed, by now."

Aaron scowled. "Hey. I said I was sorry. Why are you giving me a hard time?"

"Why are you giving *Sherry* a hard time? You're not even married yet, and you're already playing games."

"So I'm a little late."

"You're not a little late. You're nearly two *hours* late. And you come skulking in all shifty-eyed and apologetic like you did something wrong."

Aaron's mouth fell open. "You think there's another woman?"

"No. I think there's another *man.*"

His eyes faltered. "Oh."

"Come on. Fess up."

Aaron stuck the plate in the microwave, set it on HIGH for a minute and a half, and pressed START. He heaved a sigh. "Dennis is in the Country Kitchen."

"Did you confront him?"

"No."

"You just spied on him?"

"I don't want him coming here. Bothering

Sherry."

Cora looked at him in exasperation. "You idiot. *He* isn't bothering Sherry. *You* are. You let Dennis get to you, it's as bad as letting Dennis get to her. Worse, really. It just drives a wedge between you."

"You gonna tell her?"

"And now you're keeping secrets from her, and lying about where you've been. What an *excellent* way to start a marriage."

"What can I do?"

"You go eat your lamb shank and tell Sherry what a good cook she is. I'll take it from here."

Cora clomped through the living room muttering about being out of cigarettes, and slammed out the door. She hopped in her car, drove to the Country Kitchen.

Dennis Pride's car was out front. Cora pulled up next to it. She didn't really expect to find a samurai sword in the trunk. But she intended to check it out.

It was dark where Dennis had parked. Cora couldn't see in the windows. She tried the driver's-side door. It opened. Quietly. The code alarm, if any, was turned off.

With the overhead light, Cora could see there was nothing on the front seat, nothing on the floor.

She opened the rear door, checked the

backseat. Nothing.

The glove compartment beckoned. Of course, there was no way a samurai sword could be hiding there, so Cora had no excuse for snooping. Except curiosity. She opened the glove compartment, pawed through. She found nothing of interest, just a few automotive receipts and bills.

Cora closed the glove compartment, searched for the trunk release. It was on the floor. She pulled it, heard a satisfying click. She got out of the car, lifted the lid of the trunk.

The car had a trunk light, good in that she could see, bad in that there was nothing there. In the spare tire well? Not a sword. Cora checked it anyway, to no avail.

Cora closed the trunk, went to lock the door.

A cloud moved. Moonlight bathed the car.

The rear window on the driver's side gleamed bright. Like it was cleaner than the rest. Cora looked closer. It was clean indeed. As if someone had washed this window and not the others. Which wouldn't happen. You might wash the windshield and not the others. But the back window? No way.

Cora frowned. Something clicked in the back of her brain. The same sort of gift that made her so good at putting numbers in columns.

Automotive receipts.

Cora got back in the car, opened the glove compartment. Pulled out the bills and leafed through. She hadn't kept them in order. Not that Dennis was apt to notice. Still, she'd mixed them up. The one she wanted wasn't on top. It was the third one she came to.

It was a bill from Acme Auto Glass for a driver's-side rear window installed that very morning.

CHAPTER 20

"I got good news, Dennis."

Dennis Pride looked up from his scotch and soda. It was clearly not his first. He saw Cora Felton, scowled. "What are you doing here?"

"I could ask the same of you. I have a right to be in this town. You don't."

"Is Sherry here? I don't see Sherry here. The law says a hundred yards."

"And I know you're such a stickler for the law, Dennis. Relax. I told you, I got good news."

"What's that?"

"I'm not turning you in for robbery."

"What?"

"Absolutely not. I'm not even going to suggest it to the police. I won't tell them you're a suspect. Of course, if they find out on their own, it's not my fault, there's nothing I can do."

"What the hell are you talking about?"

"The samurai sword you stole from Meachem's Antique Shop. I'm not going to tell anyone you took it."

"Hey, what are you trying to pull?"

"Nothing. I told you. I'm not turning you in."

"Keep your voice down!"

"Why? You didn't do anything."

"No, but you're talking crazy. Someone might get the wrong idea."

"How can they get the wrong idea? I'm saying you *didn't* steal it."

"Shhh!"

"What's the matter. You *want* people to think you stole it?"

"Damn it!" Dennis hissed. "I didn't steal any samurai sword!"

"*Samurai* sword? How did you know it was a *samurai* sword?"

"You *said* so!"

"I didn't say it was a *samurai* sword."

"You did, too!"

"I assure you I didn't. But don't worry. Nobody's going to double-check you. Your secret's safe with me."

Dennis was beside himself, torn between shouting at her and keeping his voice down. *"You* said it was a samurai sword! I didn't know until *you said so!"*

Cora grimaced, shook her head. "No, no,

no. You're really no good at lying. Surprising, since you've been married twice. But the fact is you stink. The question isn't whether I *said* it's a samurai sword. It's whether you *think* it is. And you clearly *do.* You're a bad liar, and you blew it. But don't worry, I won't tell a soul."

"Damn it!"

Cora pulled the auto glass receipt from her purse, smoothed it out on the bar. "Bad move, keeping this receipt. It's dated, for chrissake. It has the name of the auto glass company that installed your rear window. The evidence indicates you stole the sword from the antique shop, but you were so drunk you left it in the backseat of your car, and someone smashed the glass and took it. That's what I'm guessing, and it is, by the way, the *charitable* explanation for your actions. The *un*charitable explanation, the one I'm *not* guessing, is the one where you steal the sword, use it for some nefarious purpose, such as impaling some poor son of a bitch who looked at you funny. When you sobered up you were horrified at what you'd done, figured you'd better start covering your tracks. So you smashed the back window of your car, had it repaired, and left the receipt in your glove compartment. In case someone saw you steal the sword —

which was a distinct possibility since you were drunk at the time and didn't take great precautions — you could claim you had it but someone broke your window, stole it out of your car."

Dennis wet his lips. Couldn't think of anything to say.

Cora smiled at him.

"So, aside from that, how are you?"

CHAPTER 21

Cora had the feeling she was being watched. It was an eerie feeling. She'd had it once before, when someone was stalking her. She was sure this time was different, that it was just a feeling, brought on by God knows what. Even so, when she left the bar, she could have sworn someone was there.

Cora pulled her cigarettes out of her purse, lit one up, took a deep drag. Told herself she was being stupid. Yeah, stupid for smoking. But for being on guard?

She glanced surreptitiously around, saw no one. Which didn't mean no one was there.

Or didn't mean anyone was.

Cora composed herself, started across the parking lot.

A car pulled in and Hideki got out. He didn't see her, just went up the steps of the Country Kitchen.

Cora wondered if he might have smashed

Dennis's back window and stolen a samurai sword. Did wondering that count as racial profiling? Maybe. If so, she was sorry. The thought was enough to keep her from searching his car.

That and the fact he'd locked it.

Damn. Where was a cop when you needed one?

Cora tried to peer through the rear window. Hideki had parked under the streetlight; even so she couldn't see the floor. Nor could she get into the trunk, which would have been *her* first choice to stash a stolen samurai sword.

Cora went back into the Country Kitchen.

First Selectman Iris Cooper came out of the dining room and swooped down on her. That was the problem with being a celebrity. People knew you. Not exactly a plus for a PI.

Cora stalled Iris off by promising to play bridge later in the week. She watched the first selectman go out the door, then she peered into the bar.

From the look of things, Hideki had just ordered a martini, shaken, not stirred, in finest James Bond tradition. At the far end of the bar, Dennis Pride seemed more interested in his scotch and soda than anything else. He either hadn't noticed

Hideki's presence, or didn't care. There were half a dozen bar stools between the two men, most of them occupied. No reason for either man to notice the other. Still, if Hideki had stolen the guy's sword, he might be somewhat wary of him. Unless he'd stolen it from the backseat without knowing whose car it was.

And if Dennis *had* had a sword stolen from his car, wouldn't that make him wary of Hideki? Or would he, too, be reluctant to stoop to racial profiling? Somehow, Cora doubted Dennis would possess such scruples. More than likely he was brooding into his drink, and hadn't even noticed Hideki was there.

Cora glanced up and spotted the private eye.

He was sitting at the far end of the bar. A nondescript businessman in a suit and tie, nursing his drink. A perfectly ordinary addition to a restaurant bar. Nothing out of the ordinary, nothing alarming, nothing to put one on one's guard. Cora only noticed him because he looked away. That was his one mistake.

It could have been simple eye avoidance, but it wasn't. Cora knew the difference. In the course of her many marriages, affairs, flirtations, and everything in between, Cora could spot a simple eye avoidance as well as the next gal. She knew the difference between that and someone who had been caught red-handed and was checking her out. More than one husband had put private detectives on her trail, hoping to limit the amount of the alimony; Cora made short work of them. There was one poor soul she had finessed out of his car keys and his wallet. Rather embarrassing for the unfortunate man when the police responded to her anonymous 911 call.

The guy at the end of the bar didn't look anything like that slob. But they had the same moves.

Cora felt a sudden rush of adrenaline. Excellent. She wasn't losing it. Her instincts were right after all. She was back on her game. She could feel her mind racing.

The guy was a gumshoe, that made sense. But Cora didn't think he was after her. He'd been watching her, sure, because she was there. But she wasn't the primary target. That made no sense. Who'd pay somebody to watch her?

Hideki, on the other hand, filled the bill. Two rivals trying to one-up each other. It's only logical that one might hire a PI.

Cora frowned.

Except for one thing.

She had felt she was being watched *before* Hideki drove in. That made no sense. Unless the PI anticipated his arrival, got there first. In which case he would have to know Hideki's schedule. Was that possible? Not likely. Then why was he there?

As Cora was wondering that, a young woman came in from the dining room. Lithe, slim, attractive, in tan cashmere sweater and gray velvet pants. She looked so different than she had wearing yards and yards of silk that Cora didn't recognize her until she skipped up to the bar, threw her arms around Hideki, and kissed him on the cheek.

Of course. That's why the PI was there before Hideki. He was following Hideki's wife.

But why was *she* there? She hadn't come in with her husband. She was already there when he arrived.

As if on cue, Aoki Yoshiaki came in from the dining room.

Uh-oh.

Reiko had been out with Aoki. Hideki had unexpectedly shown up. Was Aoki smooth enough to pretend he was there alone?

He wasn't about to. Aoki strode right up and stood glaring at Hideki, jaw to jaw.

Dennis, roused from the moody contemplation of his liquor, pushed away from the bar, lurched over, and stuck his finger in Aoki's chest. "You!" he declared. "You keep away from my wife!"

Hideki, greatly amused, laughed in Aoki's face.

Reiko threw her hands in the air, and stormed off.

Hideki waggled his finger at Aoki, grinned in fiendish delight, and followed Reiko out.

Aoki flung Dennis aside, and charged after his rival.

Dennis crashed into a table and fell to the floor amid a shower of silverware. As he staggered to his feet, Cora realized he was even drunker than she had thought. He took a second to get his bearings, then made for the door.

Oddly enough, the PI also decided it was time to be going.

The bar had emptied out in seconds. The bartender looked nonplused.

"Probably something you said," Cora told him.

Outside, Dennis was fumbling with his keys, trying to unlock the door of his car. He didn't seem to be having much success.

A Japanese soap opera was taking place on the far side of the parking lot. As there were no subtitles, Cora could not tell what was being said, but she could imagine.

The private eye was headed in the opposite direction, most likely to his car. Cora hesitated a moment, torn. A juicy love triangle was hard to ignore, but she knew who the players were. The gumshoe was the mystery guest.

Cora tried to appear casual and not be seen, which, it occurred to her, were diametrically opposed. If you weren't seen, how could you appear casual? Method acting, Cora rummaged in her purse for her keys as she followed the PI across the lot.

Behind her, car doors slammed, engines roared, and headlights popped on.

The PI picked up the pace, practically sprinted for his car.

Cora followed.

Prayed it would be light enough to see the license plate.

It wasn't.

The PI's nondescript American car was parked in the shadows. The license plate wasn't visible at all.

The PI started the car, switched on the lights.

Hot damn!

He had a license plate light.

It was a New York plate. As he backed up, Cora could see the number.

Of course she'd never remember it. One of the joys of getting old. Cora dug in her purse, came out with a pen and a piece of paper.

The pen didn't work. Cursing, she thrust it back in her purse, with the other pens that didn't work, and fumbled for another usable one, all the time reciting the license plate number in her head. She found a pencil that broke, another pen that didn't work (possibly the same one), finally a stubby, gnarled nub of a pencil with a little exposed lead. She scribbled the number, 99 percent sure she'd gotten it right.

By the time she was done, the Japanese trio and Dennis and the detective were long gone.

Cora went back in the Country Kitchen and called the police.

CHAPTER 22

Chief Harper looked sick to his stomach, not surprising since he'd been called back to his office late in the evening, and was slugging down the remnants of the sludge that passed for coffee in the police station urn. Still, it might have been what Cora had just told him.

"Do you know in how many ways I don't like this?"

"I can imagine a few."

"I should think you would. You have no hard evidence, only assumptions."

"You could pick him up on suspicion."

"Suspicion of what? Getting a car window fixed? Having long hair?"

"You could put him in a lineup. See if Mrs. Clemson could identify him."

"How's she going to identify him? All she saw was his hair."

"Isn't that enough?"

"You want me to put him in a lineup with

four guys with short hair, see if she picks him? That's going to be conclusive."

"So put him in a lineup with four guys with long hair."

"Sure. You know any rock bands in town? There aren't any, outside of the high school. You want me to put him in a lineup with four high school kids? His attorney would have a field day with that."

"What about the PI?"

"What about him?"

"Wouldn't you like to know who he is?"

"Why do I feel like I'll get in trouble if I do?"

"He's from New York. Probably Manhattan."

"What makes you say that."

"The other one was."

Harper groaned. "I don't like what you've been saying, and that I like least. You're saying maybe he's taking over for the dead PI?"

Cora shrugged. "Where there's a dead PI there's a career opportunity."

"That I would not like at all. It would mean his job security was poor at best."

"Anyway, wouldn't you like to know who he is?"

"You found out?"

"No, but you can. Here's his license number."

"How'd you get his license number?"

"I managed to be out in the parking lot when he left."

"When was that?"

"When Hideki and his wife drove off."

"He followed her?"

"Among others."

"He followed someone else?"

"No. He was among the people *following* Hideki and his wife."

"What do you mean?"

"Dennis Pride followed them, too."

"Dennis? Why?"

"Maybe he wanted his samurai sword back."

"Do you have any grounds for making that statement?"

"I don't have any grounds for making *any* of these statements. I certainly wouldn't want to be quoted on them. Or on any of the assumptions I've been making."

"Such as?"

"Such as Aoki hired the private eye to keep tabs on Hideki."

"I thought the private eye was there when Hideki came in."

"Yeah, but his wife was already there."

"That's somewhat convoluted."

"What?"

"The private eye hired to tail a guy instead

tails his wife."

"Look. I just got there myself. So I'm making deductions."

"No kidding."

"I'm just saying it's not as illogical as you make it seem."

"What's logical about it?"

"Okay, say the PI tails Hideki and his wife to the Country Kitchen. They go in and order drinks. Hideki says, 'Oh, hell, I left my wallet at the b-and-b. Stay here, I'll go get it.' The detective, not wanting to tail him there and back, hangs out at the bar. Mrs. Hideki goes to the can, spots Aoki in the dining room, and, being the biggest flirt this side of Tokyo joins him for dessert. Meanwhile, Dennis comes in and starts drinking, I search his car and find the auto glass receipt."

Harper put up his hand. "I don't want to hear this."

"What, you think he's gonna make a complaint? I go in and have a little talk with Dennis, designed, I hope, to send him home. I come out just in time to see Hideki go in, where he is joined by his wife and followed by half the population of western Connecticut."

"You didn't follow them?"

"I would have needed a parade permit. It

was like the whole parking lot took off."

"In what order?"

"Beats me. I was busy getting the license plate number."

"So the PI was last?"

"Probably Dennis. The PI'd want to edge him out, no matter which Asian he was tailing."

"You didn't see?"

"I had to write the plate number. The pencil broke. I couldn't find one in my purse, and I had to keep repeating the damn numbers —" Cora broke off angrily. "What difference does it make? I didn't see. So sue me."

Harper frowned. "And you think the PI was hired by Aoki?"

"I have no idea. But you could start by finding out who he is." Cora tapped the license number on Chief Harper's desk. "This is the guy's car. Unless, of course, it's a rental. In which case, you might have to lean on Hertz a little. But that shouldn't be so hard for a big time police chief like you."

Harper sighed. "You know, when you walked in the door I was actually glad to see you."

CHAPTER 23

Dennis had had too much to drink. That didn't occur to him as he followed the taillights out of town. All he was thinking was that son of a bitch wouldn't get away with it. Exactly what son of a bitch was not entirely clear.

Dennis was aware the world was closing in on him. People were dogging his footsteps. Brenda. His father-in-law. Obstacles thrown in his way. Keeping him from his goals. Fame. Fortune. Happiness.

Sherry.

Dennis bit his lip hard. Tears came to his eyes. It didn't matter. He was blind drunk already. Going on instinct. Instinct that had never failed him before. Had never let him fall off the stage in the middle of a rock concert. Unless you counted the impromptu mosh pits. Still, he'd gotten back up and performed. The band members never com-

153

plained. Not to his face. At least he'd functioned.

Something in the back of his brain told him that wouldn't work here. Trees were not a mosh pit. You kept the car on the road or you didn't get an encore. Not that his mind processed the metaphor. Still, the underlying truth kept his tires on the road.

The taillights he was following disappeared.

What the hell was he doing?

Dennis pulled to a stop, cut the engine, cut the lights. A sober instinct in the midst of a drunken thought.

He peered through the windshield, wondered what he was looking for.

A light flickered up ahead.

Aha!

Dennis started the car and pulled out. The headlights came on automatically. Lit up a road to the right. Dennis took it. Wondered why.

Red taillights beckoned like glowing embers, drawing him to the fire.

He'd show them. What right did Sherry have to do this to him? Behaving like a little slut. He wouldn't have put up with it when they were married. No way. Reflecting on his good name. Which she wasn't even using. What was *that* all about? He *gave* her his name.

Dennis was lost. At least, he couldn't see the taillights anymore. He'd been driving and driving and getting nowhere. Like a kid in a bumper car. What made him think of that? He hadn't hit anything, had he? Of course not. He was doing fine.

Now if he could just figure out where he was.

He pulled off the road. Not to ask direction. Guys didn't ask directions. Not to look at the map, either. So why did he pull off the road? Was the car nearby? He could have sworn he saw taillights. But where?

Didn't matter. He'd lost them and he'd find them. He'd done it before.

How had he done it?

Kill the motor, kill the lights.

Kill, kill, kill.

He turned the engine off. The lights went out on their own. Modern cars. Take your job. Wonder they let you drive.

Now then, what the hell was he doing here?

CHAPTER 24

Becky Baldwin, looking more like a drowsy cheerleader than a high-powered attorney, pushed the blond hair out of her eyes, and smiled across her desk at Hideki Takiyama.

"You want to sue your business competitor?"

Hideki's nose twitched. Becky's one-room law office was over the pizza parlor, and the aromas had a tendency to seep up. Today's special was tomato and basil. "Yes."

"For copyright infringement?"

"That is right."

"But you don't have a copyright."

"No. That is *his* fault."

"I understand your contention." Becky took a sip from a paper cup of coffee, tried to force herself awake. She was not used to practicing law so early in the morning. Hideki had called her at home. She rolled out of bed and rushed to the office to find him waiting. "You have no legal claim to

Miss Felton's services."

"I made the appointment. He kept it. *My* appointment."

"Technically, he didn't keep your appointment. He made one of his own."

"I was first. You can ask Miss Felton. She will tell you."

Becky frowned. "This is not a strong claim."

"I do not care. I wish to make it."

"Why?"

"To show Aoki he cannot do that."

"I understand." Becky smiled. "But, if you lose, you will just be showing him he can."

"You will not do this?"

"No, I certainly will. I just want you to understand what you're getting into. This is not an easy case. I don't want you to blame me if we're not successful."

"You do not think that you can win?"

"I didn't say that. And there are different degrees of winning. A case like this has a certain nuisance value. There's a good chance his attorneys will pay us to make it go away."

Hideki shook his head. "No. I do not want to go away. I want to win."

"I understand. And I will do everything in my power to bring about that eventuality." Becky stole a glance to see if it was too much for his English. It wasn't. She went on. "But I can't take a case like this on a contingency basis. Particularly when you're unwilling to settle."

Hideki pulled out his wallet.

"Of course."

CHAPTER 25

Cora Felton woke up with a sense of dread. Not the garden variety dread, the his-head's-not-on-the-pillow-time-to-call-the-lawyers-again dread. This was a genuine sense something was wrong. Something was her fault.

Cora played the evening back in her head: Dennis, and Hideki, and his wife, and Aoki, and the private detective. Truly a bad situation. She hadn't been happy about it. She'd reported it to Chief Harper. What more could she do?

Unfortunately, she knew the answer. Chief Harper saying, "You didn't follow them?" Her reason was right on the money. It would have been farcical, one guy following another guy following another guy. Even so, she hadn't done it. And when Chief Harper mentioned that she hadn't done it, he'd sowed the seeds of paranoia, panic, and premonition, the three *P*s that spelled *dread*.

She *should* have followed them.

She was getting old.

That thought was enough to get her out of bed and into the bathroom splashing water on her face. She looked at her reflection in the glass, told herself nothing was wrong. Hoped it was true. With Dennis Pride wandering around drunk, anything was possible.

Cora tiptoed down the hall, poked open the door to her niece's room. Sherry and Aaron were in bed. There was no reason to wake them. Cora closed the door quietly.

Buddy came scampering down the hall, yipping to be let out and fed, though in what order the little poodle was never sure. As usual, he spun in circles before leaping out the open door. He was back moments later, skidding into the kitchen for breakfast.

Cora was already having hers. A glass of orange juice and a cigarette. Cora wasn't big on cooking. If Sherry wasn't up, Cora went out. She put some kibble in a bowl, added some canned glop that smelled like tuna, marveled that a little dog could eat so much.

"That was good, huh, Buddy?"

Cora dropped her cigarette in the remains of her orange juice, and went out the door.

She drove straight to Cushman's Bakeshop, had a skim latte with two shots of espresso, and a chocolate brioche. The world immediately looked better.

Not only was Cora not to blame, but there was nothing to be blamed for. Everything was going fine. No matter how many publishers were fighting over her bod. Actually, Cora liked the idea of dueling suitors. Bod was wishful thinking. Too bad they were just after her mind.

Cora got back in the car, hung a right and cruised past the Wicker Basket, idle in the neutral zone between breakfast and lunch, and the post office, typically busy in the mid-morning as the three cars parked outside would attest. She circled the block, came out by the pizza parlor and Becky Baldwin's law office. She hung a right onto Main Street.

It occurred to Cora that her circuitous route had avoided the police station. Not that she didn't want to talk to Chief Harper. But she'd told him everything last night. No need to rehash it. He was a busy man. She was being considerate. She wasn't afraid he'd get on her for not following the detective. She just drove that way for a change.

That was the same reason she was driving past the Tastee Freez. Just for the hell of it.

161

She didn't expect anyone to be there.

Someone was.

There was a car parked out front. With a New York license plate. A nondescript, dark gray Chevy sedan, maybe three or four years old.

Oh, hell.

It had been dark when Cora searched Dennis's car. She couldn't really see it well. It could have been this car, but she couldn't be certain. Was the rear window new? It was harder to tell in the sunlight. All the panes seemed to shine.

Cora approached the car with caution. Someone might be sleeping in the seat. Someone who wasn't happy to see her. The thought made her fumble for her gun. Not that she'd ever shoot Dennis; still, he wouldn't be the first man she'd aimed at with no real intention to shoot.

All in all, Dennis sleeping it off in the front seat seemed the best of all possible worlds.

There was no one in the front seat. No one in the back. The car was empty.

The keys were in the ignition.

Well, that made it easier.

Cora opened the driver's-side door.

The wail of the car alarm made her jump back. She commented on the sound, described car alarms in general and this one in particular, and ascribed to them actions not usually undertaken by inanimate objects. She leaned into the car, took out the keys. Jabbed the button on the zapper to kill the alarm.

Cora checked the glove compartment. There was no window glass receipt. Of course, she'd given it to Dennis. But the other receipts were also missing.

The car registration form Cora found under the driver's instruction manual shed some light on the subject. The car was registered to Lester Mathews of New York City.

Cora sucked in her breath. Served her right. She'd written down the detective's license number. She'd given it to Chief Harper, but she should have remembered it. If she was on top of her game, she would have.

It occurred to Cora this evened things up. The first time there was a body and no car. This time there was a car and no body.

She'd better check.

Cora walked around the back of the Tastee Freez and stopped dead.

A man lay faceup on the pavement.

Sticking out of his chest was a samurai sword.

Two pieces of paper were impaled on it.

One was a crossword puzzle.
The other was a sudoku.

Across

1. "_____ Caesar's ghost!"
6. Strikebreaker
10. "Please," dog style?
14. Exasperated cry
15. Choir voice
16. "Shakespeare in Love" prop

17. Blank look
18. Part I of message
20. Game show host
22. FedEx notation
23. News office
26. Évian, e.g.
27. Big lug
28. Bribery
31. Olympic skater Cohen
36. Part II of message
38. Christmas toymakers
39. Cold-cuts section
40. Gets high
42. They can be choppy
43. Elem. school subject
45. Part III of message
47. Busybody
48. Lady's garment
49. Hué holiday
50. Swear words?
52. Detroit team
54. Low-altitude clouds
58. _____ B. Anthony
60. End of message
62. Dreadlocks wearer
66. All-star game side
67. Baby kangaroo
68. _____ Park (Colorado)
69. "What a shame!"
70. Added conditions

71. Words of recognition

Down

1. Beetle juice?
2. Stoolie
3. Eon section
4. Come to terms
5. Christmas pageant trio
6. On one's rocker?
7. You're looking at one
8. Bank robot
9. Appear out of the blue
10. Castoff from an ice shelf
11. Church area
12. Hold your horses?
13. Clark of the Daily Planet
19. Wipe out
21. Half Miss Muffet's fare
23. Celebration at the ballpark
24. "Yoo-hoo!"
25. Land, as a fish
26. Jelly for heating
29. Historic dress designer for Mrs. Reagan
30. Knack
32. "And let me add"
33. Graceful and slim
34. Thrower
35. Good points

37. Catcher's glove
41. Chips off the old flock?
44. Western Hispaniola
46. Vail, for one
51. Presley's "_____ Ever?"
53. Grind the teeth
54. One foot forward
55. Siamese, now
56. You may take it lying down
57. Dilettantish
58. Haul for huskies
59. 180° turns, slangily
61. Family head
63. Farm home
64. Ball peg
65. Equus asinus

			6				9	
				5	8	7		
		1						
9		6		8				1
5			3				4	
		4					7	
6	8			7			5	
				6		4		
		3			9		2	

CHAPTER 26

Cora burst in the door of Sherry's bedroom. "Get up! Get up!"

Sherry sat up in bed, pulled the sheet to her neck. "What the hell are you doing?" she demanded.

Aaron blinked groggily. "Cora?"

"Get up! Get up! We got troubles!"

"I'm not dressed," Sherry protested.

"I'm not shocked," Cora said. "Come on, come on! Get up!"

Sherry looked from Aaron to Cora. "This is ridiculous. If either one of you left I could get dressed."

"Fine. Meet me in the office. I'll be destroying the scanner."

"What?"

Minutes later Sherry padded barefoot into the office to find Cora fumbling at the scanner.

"How do you start this? Isn't there an ON switch?"

"Not like you mean. You run it through the computer. What are you trying to scan?"

"A crossword puzzle."

Sherry lifted the lid of the scanner. "Why is it ripped?"

"Don't start with me."

"Cora, what's going on?"

"I need you to copy this, solve it, and bring it to me."

"Are you out of your mind?"

"Yes. I'm losing it. It's all coming apart on me. I need this, and I need this fast."

"You're not going to show it to anybody?"

"The copy? Are you out of your mind?"

Sherry whisked the puzzle out of the scanner, fed it into the fax machine, hit COPY. "This is faster. It's not as good quality."

"I don't care. You could do it on toilet paper. Just do it. I need to know what it says before the cops ask me."

"Why are the cops going to ask you?"

"They're funny that way." Cora grabbed the original. "Solve it and meet me at the Tastee Freez."

Sherry frowned. "Isn't that the crime scene?"

"It sure is. Bring that boyfriend of yours."

"Why?"

"He'll be pissed if you don't. And you need his car."

Cora slammed out the door, hopped in the Toyota, roared down the driveway. She sped back to the Tastee Freez, praying she'd be in time.

She wasn't.

The cops were there.

CHAPTER 27

The channel 8 news team was trying to interview Chief Harper, with little success. Rick Reed, clueless on-camera reporter, wasn't swift enough to formulate a coherent question, and Harper wasn't volunteering anything.

"But it's a murder?" Rick persisted.

Chief Harper shrugged. "I'm not a medical examiner. It's not my place to say."

"Well, how was he found?"

"By Dan Finley on routine mid-morning drive-around."

"Well, in what position was the body in? Was there a murder weapon present?"

"Again, you use the word *murder*. You can't have a murder weapon without a murder."

"And you don't have a murder?"

"It's not my place to make that determination at this time." Chief Harper noticed Cora Felton driving up. "Excuse me," he told Rick Reed, and descended on the Toyota. "Cora. Thank goodness you're here. I need your help."

Cora blinked. It was a moment of truth. Cora had to admit to stealing the puzzle.

Or not.

If Cora admitted to stealing the puzzle, she could produce it, replace it, tap-dance around not being able to solve it.

It would be sticky. If the puzzle was discovered on the sword, Cora could stall until Sherry got there, and find some way to use the completed puzzle to copy from. But under the scrutiny afforded a pilfered puzzle? Unless she could come up with an explanation for it fast, there was no way to solve it under Chief Harper's nose. After all, this was a murder, the puzzle was evidence, concealing evidence was a crime. Cora was an outstanding citizen, who could never resort to anything illegal.

She had to own up to finding the body.

Cora took a breath. "What happened?" she said, and sealed her fate.

"We got another one."

"Another body?"

"You knew?"

"Three police cars, an ambulance, and the medical examiner. At the same crime scene. It's déjà vu all over again."

174

"Yeah, it's a zoo," Harper said.

"How'd channel eight get here so soon?"

"I don't know. I think Dan tips 'em off."

"He found the body?"

"Uh-huh." Harper led Cora around to the back. "Who tipped you off, Cora?"

"Saw it on TV."

"Really? They just got here."

"I guess it was a lead-in from the studio."

"Oh."

Cora exhaled, realized she'd been holding her breath. Chief Harper wasn't suspicious, just making small talk.

They came around the side of the Tastee Freez to find the body of the detective on the ground.

"Hell, right in the same place," Cora said.

"You ain't seen nothing yet," Harper told her.

Dr. Barney Nathan was kneeling over the body, blocking their view.

"Don't tell me he's missing half his face?"

"No." Harper dragged Cora to the side, pointed. "How do you like that?"

Cora gasped. "Is that a *samurai* sword?"

"That would be my guess. You happen to recognize the gentleman?"

"Yeah. That's the private eye I told you about last night. The one I suggested might make trouble."

Chief Harper leveled his finger. "Don't you dare."

"Dare what, Chief? I'm not blaming anyone. Just because I reported the guy. There's no reason you had to act on it."

Chief Harper sputtered in protest.

Cora said, "Hmm, he seems to have known he was being stabbed."

"Yeah, that sort of thing is apt to grab your attention."

"I mean his hands. Wrapped around the blade. Sliced to the bone. Shows the guy wasn't knocked out first and then stabbed. The sword wasn't an afterthought. It was the main weapon."

"I'm sure Barney will come to that conclusion. You happen to notice the paper on the sword?"

"I'm trying not to."

"Why?"

"If it's a crossword puzzle, I'm going to freak out. A person can't get killed in this damn town without a crossword puzzle involved."

"You find that unlikely?"

"No kidding. If I read it in a book, I'd throw the damn thing across the room."

"I agree. Except for one thing."

"What's that?"

"You. You live here. You attract crossword-related people. When they don't like each other, people die."

"You're telling me it *is* a crossword puzzle?"

"Not quite."

"Can I see it?"

"Just as soon as Barney's done. He gets cranky when I interrupt his crime-scene examinations."

Chief Harper had spoken out loud. The dapper doctor turned his head. "Would you prefer I withheld my preliminary finding until I get him back to the morgue?"

"Of course not, Barney. You and the gentleman carry on."

"So what is it?" Cora demanded.

"It's a sudoku puzzle."

"You're kidding."

"Wish I were."

"Is it done?"

"No. That's why I'm glad to see you." Harper flushed. "I don't mean that how it came out. I mean in terms of the investigation. I need you to solve it."

Cora frowned. "Why?"

"It's been left as a clue."

"A clue to what?"

"If I knew that, I wouldn't need to solve it. Can you solve it for me?"

"Of course."

"So what's the problem?"

"It's just numbers. It won't tell you any-thing."

"I don't care. I want it done."

"You're going to have to take it off the sword."

"I can't do that."

"Why not?"

"It's evidence. It's got to be processed as evidence."

"Okay. So when you get a copy, I'll solve it. Not that it's going to do you any good."

"Are you sure you can solve it?" Harper asked.

"I imagine half the people in America can solve it. These things are the rage."

"Good. Hey, Barney. You gonna move the body with the sword stuck in?"

"Not unless you got some way to im-mobilize it. It'll bounce around in the ambulance and cut the guy in two."

"Nice image, Barney."

"Well, what do you want me to say? It's not like I get a samurai sword killing every other week. This happens to be my first."

"Are you prepared to remove the sword from the body?"

"If I say yes, you'll tell me it's evidence, and you don't want me to touch it."

"I don't want you to mess up any fingerprints that might be on it. But you think you could ease it out of the wound?"

"I'll have to pry his fingers off it first. The blade's imbedded in the bone. Hell of a way to go."

"Yeah. Hey, Dan!" Chief Harper and Cora came around the side of the ice cream parlor to find the young officer chatting with the channel 8 news team. "Dan!"

Dan Finley came trotting up. "Yeah?"

"Get an evidence bag big enough for a slide trombone. We'll use it for the sword."

"I'm not sure we got one."

"I don't care if we use a body bag, come up with something."

Aaron Grant's Honda pulled up behind the news van. The young reporter looked peeved as he got out. Cora knew how he felt. TV had scooped him again.

Sherry hurried over to her aunt.

"You got it?" Cora whispered.

"Yeah."

"Slip it in my drawstring purse."

"*You* slip it in your drawstring purse." Sherry surreptitiously stuck the folded paper in Cora's hand.

Aaron Grant pushed his way up. "The TV guys are freaking out. They can't go back there. What's the score?"

"Well, you didn't hear it from me —"

Cora began.

"Then who did I hear it from?" Aaron interrupted.

"Take it easy," Sherry said. "Cora's only trying to help."

"Sorry. Never mind the source. What's the scoop?"

"The dead man out back's got a samurai sword sticking in his chest."

"What?!"

"That's right. And I have it on good authority the camera crew isn't gonna get a shot of it when they bring out the body, because Barney Nathan is going to remove it and Dan Finley is going to put it in an evidence bag. So, unless Rick couldn't-find-his-nose-with-two-hands-and-a-map Reed happens to stumble over the right question, channel eight viewers aren't going to know a thing about a samurai sword till they read your account in the *Gazette*."

If anything was going to lift Aaron's spirits, scooping TV should have been it. But it occurred to Cora he didn't look all that pleased. A sad commentary on the state of his impending marriage.

"Finley's going to have the sword," Cora said. "It might be good to create some sort of diversion so that channel eight doesn't cop to it."

"Fine," Aaron said. "Who's the victim?"

"Appears to be a private eye from New York."

Aaron's mouth fell open. "You're kidding!"

"No."

"But . . ."

"But what?"

"So was the first one."

"Yes."

"Killed here."

"Well, at least dumped here."

"But that doesn't make any sense."

"I don't make the facts, I just find them," Cora said. "Uh-oh, here comes the body."

An EMS team wheeled a gurney around the side of the Tastee Freez. To the disappointment of channel 8, the body was covered by a sheet. There was clearly nothing sticking out of the chest.

The gurney bumped right by Dan Finley, returning from the police car with a construction-size black plastic garbage bag.

"Well," Cora said. "Looks like you lucked into a natural diversion." She turned, trotted behind Dan Finley back to the crime scene.

Chief Harper stood gingerly holding the hilt of the sword with plastic gloves. "What have you got there? I said evidence bag, not trash bag."

"Best I could do, Chief. Unless you want me to drive to Danbury."

"If I put the murder weapon in a trash bag, the defense attorney will have a field day in court."

"They'll never know," Cora said.

Still complaining, Chief Harper began the process of putting the murder weapon in Dan Finley's trash bag.

Cora Felton stepped up to inspect the crime scene.

A chalk line had been drawn around where the body had lain. Aside from that, there was little to see. Cora didn't care.

Around the far side of the body, near the edge of the lot, a deep embankment ran off through the bushes into the woods.

Cora stole a glance at Chief Harper and Dan Finley. Their intention was fixed on getting the sword into the bag. There was no one else in sight.

Cora spun around as if her ankle had turned. She shrieked, and, arms flailing, flung herself backward down the bank.

The underbrush broke her fall. It also scratched her face, tore her clothes, and snagged her drawstring purse.

Cora plunged her hand into her purse, and came out with the crossword puzzle.

Not the copy Sherry had solved. The original, unsolved puzzle with the jagged tear.

With the puzzle in her hand, Cora righted herself, scrambled toward the bank.

Chief Harper and Dan Finley appeared above her.

"My God, are you all right?" Harper cried.

Cora flashed him her trademark smile. She wondered how it looked from above. "Couldn't be better." She thrust the crossword puzzle over her head. "Look what I found."

CHAPTER 28

"You touched it," Chief Harper said.

"Of course I touched it. How was I going to pick it up if I didn't touch it."

"But, but, but . . ."

"Come on, Chief. I fell on a piece of paper. I picked it up and looked at it. It was this. If I'd known in advance it was this, I could have avoided touching it. But my powers of omniscience are not what they used to be."

"Could you not touch it anymore?"

"Sure. You'll notice I'm holding it by my thumb and forefinger. If you have an evidence bag, I'd be glad to slip it in." Cora smiled. "Perhaps a small kitchen garbage bag?"

"Dan?"

"I gotta ditch the murder weapon, Chief."

"I hope nobody heard you say that."

Dan locked the samurai sword in the trunk of his police car, came back with an evidence bag. Cora slipped the crossword puzzle in.

"Fine," Chief Harper said, drily. "Now that we've preserved your fingerprints, is there anything you'd like to tell us?"

"You note this puzzle is ripped?"

"I do."

"And there are two types of perforation. In the middle of the puzzle there's a short, clean cut, as if it had been stuck on the sword. And the other perforation, extending from the edge of the straight cut to the edge of the paper, is jagged and irregular."

"From which you infer?"

"The same thing you do. The crossword puzzle and the sudoku were impaled on the sword and the sword was plunged into the victim. The sudoku stayed stuck to the sword. The crossword puzzle tore free."

"Why?"

Cora shrugged. "I don't know. I've never stabbed anyone with a sword with a paper impaled on it. But if the guy didn't want to be stabbed — it might surprise you how few people do these days — in the course of resisting he might have torn the puzzle loose. There's some evidence he resisted in the fact he tried to pull the sword out of his chest."

"Then why isn't the crossword puzzle

bloody?"

"Huh?"

"If he pulled it off the sword. I mean, look at his hands."

"I'm assuming he pulled it off *before* slicing his fingers to the bone."

"Really? If you had a sword in your chest, would you pull the paper off it first, or try to take it out? What's your theory there?"

"My theory is he tried to avoid having the sword *put* in his chest. In flailing to avoid that, he dislodged the puzzle."

"I suppose," Harper said.

"What's the matter?" Cora asked.

"I liked it better with just the sudoku."

"What do you mean?"

"Well, you've got the Japanese publishers in town. And you've been asked to do a sudoku book. The sudoku is a nice touch. The crossword puzzle seems like overkill."

Cora's eyes widened. "Are you suggesting I threw in a crossword puzzle of my own just because I was disappointed to find a sudoku?"

"I'm not saying that."

"Well, what *are* you saying?"

"I'm not sure."

"Well, let me know if you figure it out," Cora said. "Meanwhile, when you get the evidence processed, send me copies of the puzzle and the sudoku. By then you'll have a lot more information. Maybe we can figure out what this is all about."

Cora went to look for Sherry. Rick Reed tried for an interview, but Cora waved him off. "I got nothing for you, Rick. Not even a good 'no comment.' "

Cora found Sherry standing by the road looking forlorn. "Where's Aaron?"

"He went back to the paper to write up the story."

"You didn't tag along?"

"He's working."

"You've tagged along before."

"Yeah."

"You're saying I shouldn't ask?"

"Does the word *butt out* ring a bell?"

"That's two words. As I'm sure you know."

A car pulled up and Brenda Wallenstein exploded from it. She'd been crying and her eyeliner was running. Her red hair stuck out from the sides of her head like a circus clown's.

"Is it him?" Brenda cried. "I can't take it! You gotta tell me! Is it him?"

"You mean Dennis?" Cora said.

"Yes, Dennis. You mean it isn't? Or it is?"

"It's not Dennis," Cora said. "It's some private eye."

Brenda stopped in mid-histrionics. "Oh,

thank God! Oh, my goodness! Sherry, I'm so sorry. He didn't come home. I don't know where he is."

"When's the last you heard from him?" Cora asked.

"Yesterday morning. When he left for work. He had appointments all day. I didn't expect him until late. It got later and later. I almost called."

"Called?" Cora said.

"You. The house. I know how obsessive he gets. But I didn't. I figured he was with the boys."

"The boys?"

"The band. When he gets depressed, he sneaks off and plays with the band. It's like therapy, really."

"And you let him?" Sherry said.

Brenda's face darkened. "Oh, you're a fine one to talk. And what did *you* let him do, when *you* were his wife?"

Rick Reed, having struck out with everyone else, descended on Brenda. "And here we have Brenda Wallenstein Pride, of the Wallenstein Textiles Wallensteins. Ms. Wallenstein, what brings you all here from New York City? Had you heard of the crime?"

Brenda greeted Rick with an expletive not usually heard on television. The young reporter blanched, and veered into one of his more awkward segues, which, for Rick Reed, was saying something.

"Well done," Cora told Brenda. "I must remember that for future interviews."

"Could everyone stop joking," Brenda said. "I'm worried. Where is Dennis?"

Chief Harper came walking up just in time to encounter a seriously discombobulated Rick Reed. The reporter latched onto him like a lifeline, aiming camera, microphone, and question in his direction.

"Chief Harper. Rick Reed, channel eight news. Do you have an official statement? Can you shed some light on the situation?"

"Yes, I can. A man has been found dead. His identity is being withheld pending notification of next of kin. But it appears he is not a resident of Bakerhaven. According to the identification on the body, he's from New York City."

Brenda, despite assurances it wasn't Dennis, let out a little moan.

"The decedent appears to have met with foul play," Harper went on. "We're not ruling out murder. Though it could also have been manslaughter, or even accidental death."

"What about suicide?" Rick asked.

"I would say it was very unlikely it was suicide."

"Why do you say that?"

"Because you asked."

Rick flushed. "No, I mean —"

"That's all we have at the present time," Chief Harper said. "I'll give you an update just as soon as we get it."

Brenda descended on Chief Harper. "You said he's from New York. But it's not Dennis."

"No. It's not Dennis. Didn't Cora tell you?"

"Yes."

"I take it Dennis is missing?"

"Since yesterday."

"I'll keep an eye out. But I imagine he's home by now."

"He shouldn't be. He has work."

"You know you're not making much sense?"

"I'm upset."

"I noticed."

While they were talking a police cruiser pulled up and Dan Finley got out.

"What's he doing back?" Harper said. "He's supposed to be on his way to the lab."

Dan went around the cruiser and opened the back door.

Dennis Pride climbed out. He was unshaven, his long hair was matted and greasy, his eyes were bloodshot. His suit looked like he'd slept in it. His loosely knotted tie hung from his neck like a noose.

Dan took him by the arm, pulled him from the car.

Channel 8, slow on the uptake, had just swiveled around. The cameraman made up for it by zooming in for a nice close-up on his wrists.

Dennis was wearing handcuffs.

And there was blood on his hands.

CHAPTER 29

Chief Harper sighed and rubbed his head. "What a nightmare."

Cora tipped back in her chair and pulled the cigarettes out of her drawstring purse. "That's putting it mildly, Chief."

"You can't smoke in here."

"Yes, I can. You're in trouble and you need my help. If I can't smoke, I'll leave. Your move." She lit her cigarette, blew out the match.

Harper ignored it. "What are they doing in there?"

"Who? Becky and Dennis? Well, seeing as how he just got arrested for murder and she's a lawyer, they're probably discussing that. Of course, he could be just trying to date her up. These married men have so few morals."

"Do you think he did it?"

"No, and neither do you. You arrested him on circumstantial evidence that looks bad.

But that's it. If you came up with a motive, that would be different. But you can't, so you won't, so it's not going to fly. He's not a killer. He's a sniveling punk wife-beater. But kill someone? He wouldn't have the guts."

"Even if he was drunk?"

Cora grimaced. "That's the only joker in the deck. People do a lot of things when they're drunk. I should know. I'd have at least one less husband if it weren't for liquor." She frowned. "I suppose it's one *fewer* husband. *Less* would imply lopping off a limb or two. Which isn't that bad an idea."

"Becky's going to say charge him or release him," Chief Harper said glumly.

"So release him."

"There's too much evidence against him. He was passed out in his car a half a mile from the crime scene with blood on his hands. Plus he stole the sword."

"You don't know that."

"It's *your* theory."

"My theory is someone stole the sword from *him*."

"Even so. The prosecutor won't release him."

"Who, Ratface?"

"Do you have to call him that?"

193

"Only when he's doing something annoying. Henry Firth has a habit of doing annoying things. So he reminds me of a rat."

"You're not helping. You sit there smoking, and you're not helping."

"What do you want me to do, talk you through it? Okay, what have you got from the New York cops?"

"Not much. They checked out his office. There's nothing to indicate he was recently hired. So, we can assume he was *very* recently hired, most likely in cash, by people who wish to remain anonymous." Harper shrugged. "I suppose that would have to include Dennis."

"Yeah," Cora said sarcastically. "If you want to pay a guy a lot of money to drive out in the country so you could kill him."

"I admit I'm thin on motive."

"It's not your problem, Chief. If Henry Firth wants to prosecute, *he's* the moron."

"And I'm stuck gathering facts to bolster the case."

"And suppressing the ones that don't?"

"That's not fair."

"My point exactly."

"That's not what I meant." Harper scowled. "The problem with police work is once you a throw a lawyer into the mix it's so adversarial no one wants to back down.

You're on one side, they're on the other. The lawyer won't let the client talk. The prosecutor won't let the client go. It's a stalemate. They dig in their heels, and nothing gets done."

"Sometimes they make a deal."

"Yeah, right," Chief Harper scoffed. "Like Becky Baldwin's ever going to make a deal."

Becky came out of the interrogation room. "Henry Firth around?"

"No. Why?"

"I want to make a deal."

CHAPTER 30

Becky Baldwin smiled for the TV camera. "That's right. My client, Dennis Pride, is cooperating with the police. He's made a full statement. That's why he is being released at this time."

"I heard rumors of a plea bargain," Rick Reed said.

"You heard wrong. Dennis hasn't pled guilty to anything. All charges against him have been dropped."

"And what charges were those?"

"Good point," Becky said. "Actually, he was never charged with anything. He was detained for questioning, he cooperated fully, and he's been released."

"Then why was he promised immunity?" Rick Reed persisted.

Becky smiled. "May I ask your source?"

"That is the rumor going around. That Dennis Pride only made a statement *after* he was promised immunity."

"Which should in no way reflect on Dennis Pride," Becky said with a smile. "Look, since you've brought the matter up, I'm Mr. Pride's attorney. I wish to cooperate with the authorities just as much as he does. But, as his attorney, I cannot allow him to do anything that might jeopardize his rights. Mr. Pride is currently on probation. I can't let him do or say anything that might violate the terms of that probation. Which includes being found guilty of any misdemeanor, however minor. I therefore obtained from the prosecutor, Henry Firth, a grant of immunity from any crime, technical or otherwise, excluding murder, with which Mr. Pride might conceivably be charged. Mr. Pride made a full, frank, and open disclosure, and was released from custody."

"But what did he say?"

"I am not at liberty to divulge the details of an ongoing murder investigation. You'll have to direct your questions to Henry Firth."

"But —"

"Thank you very much," Becky said, and strode away.

"And there you have it," Rick Reed summed up. "A shocking, stunning, and dramatic statement from Dennis Pride's lawyer. A statement that leaves as many questions unanswered as . . ." Rick, lost for a conclusion, finished lamely, ". . . as it actually answers. Dennis Pride, who was not available for the interview, is back on the streets, after having been picked up for the murder of Lester Mathews. He must have had quite a story. This is Rick Reed, channel eight news."

Sherry muted the commercial.

"Quite a story, indeed. I wonder what the son of a bitch said," Aaron grumbled.

"Aaron," Sherry said.

"He's getting away with murder," Aaron said bluntly. "He's sold Becky Baldwin on some cock-and-bull story, and now she's peddling it."

"That's not fair."

"To whom? Him or Becky Baldwin."

"Becky's a smart attorney. Of course she got him immunity. That's her job."

"She didn't get him immunity for murder."

"He's not a killer."

"You don't know that."

"Aaron, you're upset. You don't like him, I get that. Don't overreact."

"I'm not overreacting. Here's a guy who beat you. Now he's arrested for murder. And *I'm* overreacting."

Cora Felton came in the front door. "Hey,

kids. What's up?"

"Nothing," Aaron muttered.

Cora shot Sherry an inquiring look.

"The police released Dennis and Aaron's upset," Sherry said.

"Yeah," Cora said. "I was there."

"What's the story?"

"Well, this is not for publication."

"Here we go again!" Aaron stormed.

"Yeah, life's not fair. We get that. Here's the scoop. Dennis is a bad boy. He's violated his probation six ways from Sunday. He comes around, he gets drunk, he obsesses on certain crossword puzzle constructors who shall be nameless. Becky's gotta get that wiped clean, and Ratface is glad to wipe it. So Becky gets immunity to everything but murder. As soon as she does, Dennis cops to stealing a samurai sword from an antique shop."

"What?!" Aaron cried.

"Turns out there's a ninety-nine percent chance that sword is the murder weapon, so it's a real good crime to have immunity on."

"But he doesn't have immunity to murder."

"No, he claims the sword was stolen from him."

"Give me a break!"

"Says it was taken from his car. Points to

a receipt from an auto glass shop to back his story."

"But he had blood on his hands."

"Yes, he did. And DNA tests will probably confirm it's the victim's blood." Cora shook her head. "But it practically screams frame-up. Dan found him passed out in his car with bloody hands. But there was no blood anywhere else. Not on the door handles. Not on the steering wheel. The car was half a mile from the crime scene. There's no way he drove it half a mile without smearing blood around. All the evidence would seem to indicate the killer found him passed out in his car, and couldn't resist trying to frame him by smearing his hands with blood."

"And I can't print any of this?" Aaron said incredulously.

"Not on my say-so. But now you know the story, there's nothing to stop you from collecting those facts on your own."

Aaron looked exasperated for a moment, then slammed out the door.

"You sure lit a fire under him," Sherry said.

"I wanted to talk to you alone. Has he been in a funk all day, or just since Dennis got out of jail?"

"He was just as gloomy when Dennis was

in. I'm tired of taking a hit for my ex."

"Dennis is more ex than most guys have to deal with." Cora flopped down on the couch. "I need a smoke. Oh, hell! I left my purse in the car."

"Did you look at the puzzle?" Sherry asked.

"Never had a chance. Lemme get my purse."

Cora heaved herself to her feet and went out the door. She was back a minute later.

"It's not there."

"What?"

"My purse. It's not in the car."

"You mean someone took it?"

"Unless I — Uh-oh!"

"What?"

"I must have left it in Chief Harper's office."

"With the puzzle in it?"

"And my cigarettes."

"I don't have another copy."

"I don't have another cigarette." Cora rubbed her head. "This is awful. If Chief Harper looks in my purse I'm screwed. *And* I'm having a nicotine fit."

"I don't think the chief's the type of guy to go through a woman's purse."

"You wanna bet your freedom on it?"

"Oh, come on."

"Well, whaddya think they do with people who tamper with evidence? Slap 'em on the wrist? At least you didn't *knowingly* do it. You're an unwitting dupe. If this blows up, *I'm* the one going to jail. The only way *you're* going to jail, is if we *both* go to jail. In which case, I'm going in disgrace as the unfrocked Puzzle Lady."

The phone rang.

Sherry padded into the kitchen, picked it up. "Hello . . . Just a minute." She covered the receiver. "It's Harper."

Cora snatched the phone from Sherry. "Hi, Chief."

"Cora. You left your purse here."

"I just realized that."

"Want to come over and get it?"

"Now?"

"Well, we got the crossword puzzle back from the lab. I thought you'd be interested."

"Oh."

"Particularly since all the fingerprints on it turn out to be yours."

"Sorry, Chief. If I'd known what it was . . ."

"Yes, of course. Anyway, you could solve it and pick up your purse at the same time."

"Solve it and pick up my purse at the same time," Cora repeated for Sherry's benefit, motioning for help.

"Fax the puzzle," Sherry said.

"Excuse me a minute, Chief. What was that, Sherry?"

"You were going to run me into town and I'm not ready yet," Sherry said loudly enough for the chief to hear. "Have him fax you the puzzle, you can solve it while you're waiting."

"Okay. Chief —"

"I heard, I heard," Harper said. "I'll fax you the puzzle."

"Can you do that?"

"Sure. What's your fax number?"

"Hang on." Cora covered the phone, hissed, "Sherry! Do we have a fax number?"

Chapter 31

Chief Harper smiled when Cora came in. "Boy, am I glad to see you."

"Sorry to take so long, Chief. I had to drop my niece over at the paper. She's having a spat with Aaron, wanted to patch things up."

Harper blinked. That was far more information than he expected. "But you solved the puzzle?"

"I have it right here, Chief, and — Oh! There's my purse!" Cora snatched it up. "Thank goodness. I've been wanting my cigarettes."

"You can't smoke in here."

"Well, I have to smoke somewhere. I'm going nuts. You know what it's like to solve a puzzle without nicotine?"

"I can't really relate to that."

"Well, trust me, it's bad. You wanna look the puzzle over, I'll go smoke outside."

"No, stay. I'm gonna want your opinion."

"On what?"

"The puzzle, of course. It's not enough to know what it says. I have to know what it means."

"We got a little problem there."

"What's that?"

Cora slapped the puzzle down on Harper's desk.

"Look at the theme entries, Chief. See

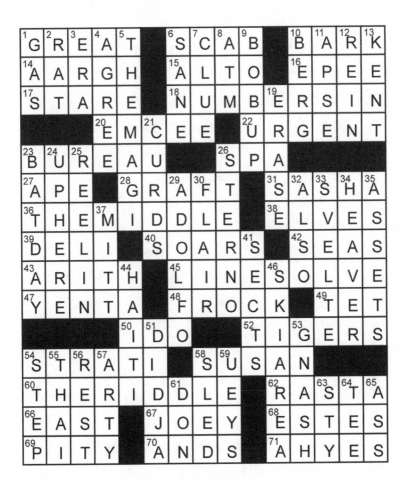

what it says? *Numbers in the middle line solve the riddle.* That would refer to the sudoku, which I haven't solved yet, since I don't have a copy."

"Got one right here."

"Fine. I'll solve it. And when I do, you know what I'm gonna get? Eighty-one squares with the numbers one through nine in them."

"Yeah, but what about the numbers in the middle line?"

"That will be the numbers one through nine in no particular order."

"What do you mean, no particular order?"

"I mean I don't know the order."

"It will be in *one* particular order?"

"What do you mean?"

"The sudoku — is there only one order the numbers can be?"

"Of course. Otherwise it wouldn't be a sudoku. A sudoku has only one solution. If it isn't unique, it's not a sudoku."

"So when you say in no particular order . . . ?"

"I'm dead wrong," Cora said irritably. "They *are* in a particular order. I just don't know what that particular order might be. I sure as hell don't know what it means."

"Let's stop talking in the abstract. You

wanna solve the thing, see what the number is."

Cora took the copy of the sudoku, filled the numbers in. It wasn't that hard. She was done in minutes.

"Good," Harper said. "If this is what the crossword means, what have we got?"

"We've got numbers. And not very interesting ones at that. Don't you wish someone would invent a new number. Like a *snurf,* somewhere between a seven and an eight." At Harper's look, Cora said, "All right, all right. You know as much as I do. Which isn't good, 'cause I don't know squat. The puzzle says the line in the middle. Sudoku have rows and columns. As well as three-by-three boxes. If it said the box in the middle, it

7	4	5	6	3	1	8	9	2
3	6	2	9	5	8	7	1	4
8	9	1	7	4	2	3	6	5
9	7	6	4	8	5	2	3	1
5	1	8	3	2	7	9	4	6
2	3	4	1	9	6	5	7	8
6	8	9	2	7	4	1	5	3
1	2	7	5	6	3	4	8	9
4	5	3	8	1	9	6	2	7

would be easy. It would be the center square. That was Paul Lynde, as I recall. Remember him? 'Why do motorcycle riders wear leather jackets? Because chiffon wrinkles in the wind.' "

"Cora."

"Sorry. But it's not a square, it's a line. Sudoku rows are horizontal, columns are vertical. So the line in the middle would be the fifth row across, the horizontal row that goes through the center square of the center square."

Harper put up his hand. "Don't start that again."

"Never fear. Anyway, that gives us what we knew all along. The numbers one through nine, scrambled in a particular order. And that order is: five-one-eight-three-two-seven-nine-four-six."

"Okay," Harper said. "What could that be?"

Cora cocked her head. "That private eye have a safe?"

CHAPTER 32

Chief Harper clicked open the door to the PI's office. "The cops aren't too happy about this."

"I like that, Chief," Cora said.

"What's that?"

"You talking about the cops as if you weren't a cop."

"I mean the New York cops."

"I know what you mean, Chief. It's still good to hear. You think we dare risk a light?"

"It's not like we broke in."

"I know. I'm just trying to get in the mood."

The private eye's office was a hole-in-the-wall affair on the Upper East Side of Manhattan just off Third Avenue. It had a barred window, which seemed excessive, since it was on the fifth floor with no fire escape, and had a police lock on the door. It occurred to Cora the PI either had something valuable in the office, or tended to piss people off.

Lester Mathews had a phone and answering machine, but no fax or computer. Apparently the guy didn't get that much work.

There was no safe in sight.

"There goes that idea," Harper said.

"Ten bucks says he's got a wall safe."

"Ten bucks?"

"I'll make it twenty."

"I'm not risking twenty bucks."

"I'll give you two-to-one odds."

"What?"

"Make it ten-to-one."

Harper frowned. "How come you're so sure."

Cora pointed. "See the calendar?"

"What about it?"

"It's two years old, and there's no naked ladies. The only reason the guy'd have an out-of-date calender that wasn't porn is if it's hiding something. Take a look. He's either got a wall safe, or a hole into the ladies' powder room."

It was a safe.

Chief Harper set the calendar aside, surveyed the combination lock.

"Okay," Cora said. "We got nine numbers here. Five-one-eight-three-two-seven-nine-four-six. That will divide up into four two-digit numbers and one one-digit number.

The first number is four full turns to the right and stop on either five or fifty-one."

"Why four full turns?"

"Because it's five numbers, and you have decreasing turns. Four full turns stop on the first number. Three full turns stop on the second number. Two full turns stop on the third number. One full turn stops on the fourth number. Part turn back to the fifth number.

"So, the first number could be five or fifty-one. The second number could be eighteen, or eight, or . . . Oh, for Christ's sake!"

"What?"

"It doesn't work."

"What do you mean?"

"The numbers on this lock only go up to forty."

"So?"

"The nine numbers can't be in the combination."

"Why not?" Harper asked.

"They're too big. The last number on the dial is thirty-nine."

"Forty."

"Yeah, but we got no zero."

"So thirty-nine's the highest number. So what?"

"So the numbers don't work. I said the first number has to be five or fifty-one. But it can't be fifty-one, because that's more than forty."

"So it's five."

"Yeah," Cora said, "but then you've used up your one-digit number, so all the rest have to be two-digit. Five-one-eight-three-two-seven-nine-four-six has to be five-eighteen-thirty-two-seventy-nine-forty-six. Five, eighteen, and thirty-two are all right, but seventy-nine and forty-six won't fly."

"You're saying this isn't the combination?"

"That's what I'm saying."

"So we're wasting our time."

"Yes, and no."

Harper looked pained. "What do you mean by that?"

"Well, I'd still like to get into that safe. The combination must be here somewhere. He isn't the type of guy to trust to memory. It's either written on that calendar, or taped to the bottom of one of the drawers in the desk. I'll take the calendar, you take the drawers."

"Oh, all right," Harper said reluctantly. With an air of doing it purely to oblige her, he began checking the bottom of the desk drawers. He was surprised to find masking tape on one, assumed it covered up some sort of crack. He pulled it off, looked, and whistled.

"What you got?" Cora asked.

"L twenty-two, R eight, L sixteen."

"That seems much more like a combination. Care to give it a whirl?"

"Yeah, but . . ."

"But what?"

"It's not helping us with the number."

"You never know, Chief. Maybe there'll be a box inside that you have to press in the numbers one through nine in a particular sequence or it explodes."

"Are you kidding?"

"I hope so. I don't need any exploding boxes, thank you very much. Let's see what we got."

Chief Harper tried the numbers, but the safe wouldn't open.

"That isn't it?" Cora said.

"I may have blown a number. You were talking."

"Right, right, it was my fault," Cora said.

"Let me try it again."

The safe clicked open.

Chief Harper reached inside. "No drawers. Just a top shelf and a bottom shelf."

"What's on the top shelf?"

"Why the top shelf?"

"Okay, what's on the bottom shelf?"

"If you're tying to annoy me, you're doing

a great job." Chief Harper pulled out a roll of bills. "Well, it would appear our decedent had close to two hundred dollars in cash. Why he elected to lock it in a safe I have no idea."

"I don't think it's fair to call a guy who got murdered paranoid."

"And on the other shelf we have . . . uh-oh."

"What is it?" Cora said, but even as Harper turned away from the wall safe she could recognize her smiling face adorning a Puzzle Lady crossword puzzle.

" 'The Puzzle Lady has some advice on how to deal with an annoying, moody ex,' " Harper read.

Across

1. "Arms and the Man" playwright
5. Fizzling out sound
9. Drop behind
14. Pants-on-fire type
15. Bern's river
16. Was priced at
17. Advice part 1

19. Yossarian portrayer
20. 1970s dance music
21. "_____ Misérables"
22. Renter's paper
23. "The Twittering Machine" artist
25. 401(k) alternative
27. Hernando's "Huh?"
30. Advice part 2
36. _____ Bator
38. Hoedown date
39. Most of Mauritania
40. Start to freeze?
41. Eniwetok event
43. Vanity cases
44. Popeye's type
46. 007, for one
47. Quaker William
48. Advice part 3
51. Run to seed
52. Mercury, Mars, Jupiter, etc.
53. Corp. chiefs
55. Pilgrim's title
59. India neighbor: Abbr.
61. Ready for drawing
65. "Your three minutes _____"
66. Advice end
68. Island near Quemoy
69. Modern ice cream flavor
70. "Make my day," e.g.
71. Gambler's routines: Abbr.

72. Central point
73. Midterm worry

Down

1. Went smoothly
2. Stereo hookup
3. Contented sighs
4. Jalopy
5. Course number
6. Did not succeed in
7. Complimentary
8. _____ O'Shea
9. Refrain from singing?
10. Pink, as a steak
11. "My Way" singer
12. "Really?"
13. Like some wolves
18. Pepsi, for one
24. Match-opening cry
26. Design differently
27. Suppress a rebellion
28. Forearm bones
29. Sup at home
31. Former Crayola color
32. Good name for aherding dog
33. Bar order
34. Home of the Maine Lobster Institute
35. "Rome _____ built in a day"

37. Luxor's river
42. Freckled
45. Complex subject?
49. Draw off
50. "Fiddlesticks!"
54. Nasty, as a remark
55. Radio amateurs
56. Without _____ of hope
57. Air travelers
58. Barely
60. Sleek, for short
62. Kodak film brand
63. Indian tourist locale
64. Frost lines
67. "The Bells" writer

"This has nothing to do with anything," Cora protested.

"How do you know that?"

"Are you kidding? It's a puzzle in a newspaper. A nationally syndicated puzzle. It doesn't mean anything special to anyone."

"Now, you don't know that. This crossword puzzle may have a deep personal meaning to some poor soul."

"Bite me."

"Anyway, I'm going to need you to solve it."

"Not this minute, you're not. This isn't

fun and games. We're tossing a dead man's digs."

Harper winced. "Where do you come up with this lingo? I'm embarrassed just hearing it."

"What else is in the safe?"

"Nothing. The guy keeps money and your picture. I'm trying hard to withhold comment."

"Hey!" Cora waggled her finger. "You better be nice, or you can solve your own damn crime."

CHAPTER 33

"What has nine numbers?" Cora said. "Come on, kids, help me here."

"Aaron's in a funk," Sherry told her.

"I'm not in a funk. I just don't understand it."

"What don't you understand?"

"A guy gets caught with a murder weapon and the police let him go."

"He wasn't caught with it," Sherry said. "He stole it."

"That's entirely different."

"Why are you defending him?"

"I'm *not* defending him. I just don't think he did it. Do you?"

"I didn't say I thought he did it."

"No. You just want him locked up. Whether he did it or not."

"Sherry —"

"Hey, hey," Cora said. "You two cut it out. Ex-husbands are a pain. I ought to know, I've had enough of 'em. Granted, none were as bad as Dennis. With the possible exception of Melvin. Anyway, you kids are never gonna get divorced. You know why? You fight too well. You're too evenly matched. You're too good at it. It would be a waste of good old-fashioned brain power. Now, that being said, shut up for a minute and give me some help."

"Help with what?"

"With the numbers. The stinking, lousy numbers. The numbers that should mean something but don't."

"I'm no good with numbers," Sherry said.

"Yeah," Aaron said. "You need a numerologist. Like the guys on the TV show."

"What TV show."

"*Numbers.*"

"They're actors."

"So?"

"They can't help me. I need a real number person. And even that won't help. I don't have to understand the number. I just have know what it is."

"Did you break it down?" Sherry said.

"How?"

"I don't know. It's nine numbers. What if it's three groups of three."

"Okay, let's try that," Cora said. "That gives me five-one-eight, three-two-seven, nine-four-six."

"Maybe it's a phone number."

"How can it be a phone number?"

"Five-one-eight is the area code. The rest is the phone number."

"That's only six numbers. A phone number's seven numbers."

"How about a zero?" Sherry suggested.

"Where?"

"I don't know. But a zero means nothing. Adding a zero wouldn't change anything."

"Adding a zero would give you the same number."

"I don't mean add it. Use it. As the seventh number."

"You can't do that."

"Why not?"

"It changes the number. Makes it ten times bigger."

"So what, if it's a phone number? Why are we arguing. Just try it."

Cora dialed the number.

"It didn't go through."

"Did you dial one first?"

"If I dialed one first, it would be two ones."

"The one you dial first doesn't count."

"The one I dial doesn't count. The zero I dial doesn't count. I'm dialing all these numbers that don't count."

"Dial it," Sherry said. "How can it hurt?"

"If I wind up with a seventy-two-dollar phone call to Australia, let's remember you said that."

The number didn't go through.

"Wanna try moving the zero?"

"I don't think we even have a valid area code."

"So, could it be a license plate number?" Aaron suggested.

"They're not that long."

"They're close to it. What's New York now? Three digits, then four more. That's seven digits."

"Some of which are letters. We're talking nine digits, all numbers. You see any license plates look like that?"

"Okay," Sherry said. "We broke it up into three groups of three. Suppose that's not it? Suppose it's two and then three and then four? Five-one, eight-three-two, seven-nine-four-six. The last seven digits could be a phone number. The first two could be something else."

"Such as what?"

"I don't know."

"Well, that doesn't look like any number I ever saw."

"How about five-one-eight, three-two-seven-nine, four-six?" Aaron said. "Like it's

223

a phone number, and forty-six is the extension?"

"Then what's the area code?"

"That's a problem."

"Wait a minute!" Cora said. "How about one of those what-chamacallits? You know, a substitution code? Where numbers stand for letters?"

Sherry shook her head. "Not long enough. Unless you had a decoder ring, you could never solve it. Not with only nine numbers, all different."

"Decoder ring?" Cora said. "Isn't that a little before your time?"

"I know words," Sherry said. "Sorry it doesn't help."

"Yeah."

Cora picked up a pencil, jotted the number down, and stared at it. "All right, you son of a bitch. What are you trying to tell me?"

CHAPTER 34

Chief Harper groped for the phone. "Hello?"

"Chief. Wake up. It's Cora."

"Who?"

"I think I got it."

"Got what?"

"Honey, what is it?"

"Go back to sleep, dear."

"I thought I heard the phone."

"You did. I got it. Go to sleep."

"Chief —"

"You woke my wife."

"I'm sorry."

"You don't know the meaning of the word."

"It's the numbers."

"What about 'em?"

"I got it."

"You know what it is?"

"I know what it must be."

"Then you *don't* know what it is?"

"I have a theory."

"Couldn't it wait till morning?"

"Sure," Cora said, and hung up.

Her phone rang a minute later.

"We got disconnected," Harper said.

"I thought we were going to wait until morning."

"I'm awake."

"I can tell."

"My wife is awake. Which means I won't be going back to sleep any time soon."

"I don't suppose you want to go into the office, either."

"What are you talking about?"

"Well, it could be a bank account number. But it isn't. At least, no bank account around here. The prefix is wrong. Of course, if it turns out to be some account in the Cayman Islands, that's another story. But, barring that —"

"Cora."

"Sorry. I drank too much coffee trying to stay awake."

"You're wired on caffeine?"

"That doesn't make me wrong."

"No. But it makes you do stupid things. Like calling me in the middle of the night."

"Sorry, Chief, won't happen again," Cora said, and hung up.

Her phone rang ten seconds later.

Cora answered, "Hello?"

"Stop hanging up the phone," Harper growled. "I got enough problems without you playing games."

"Make up your mind, Chief. You want to talk to me or not?"

"Right now I'd like to wring your neck. I'm awake. I don't wanna be. Tell me what you called to tell me, so I can get back to sleep."

"We're grouping the numbers wrong. Like bank accounts and area codes. I think I finally grouped 'em right."

"Okay. And what is that."

"Five-one-eight, three-two, seven-nine-four-six."

CHAPTER 35

The IRS agent was icy as could be. Which was hardly fair, since Chief Harper hadn't wakened him up at four in the morning, but had called him from the police station the next day. This did not please Chief Harper, nor did the fact he had Cora Felton perched on a chair in his office waiting to see how he'd do with the IRS. Striking out with a government minion in front of the Puzzle Lady was not the way the chief wanted to start his day. Even the blueberry ginger muffin from Cushman's Bakeshop wasn't enough to counteract that.

"I'm the chief of police. I'm conducting a murder investigation. I need this Social Security number traced."

The IRS agent wasn't impressed. "So you say. You're just a disembodied voice on the phone. How do I know you're even a cop?"

"Look," Harper said. "It's not like I couldn't get this information. A search engine on my computer will provide it for forty-nine dollars. I just can't justify a charge like that in my department's expenses. Some IRS agent would want to know why I am paying for information to which I am legally entitled."

"If you'd like to fill out an official request for information regarding a U.S. taxpayer, I'll require proof of identity, proof of occupation, proof of the legitimacy of the request . . ."

"Look, Norman. Excuse me, that is your name, isn't it? Norman Jenks? Extension six-four-two? I'm Chief Harper of the Bakerhaven police force. I'm investigating the murder of Lester Mathews. I'm going to hang up the phone now. Please call information, ask for the Bakerhaven police department. Call that number and ask for the chief of police. When I answer the phone, establishing that I *am* the Bakerhaven chief of police, let me know whose Social Security number this is. That way you'll be aiding a police investigation instead of obstructing one. Your lawyer can tell you the difference."

Harper hung up the phone.

"That sounded like a threat," Cora said.

"I hope he heard it that way. You really think it's a Social Security number?"

"I don't know what else it could be."

"That's hardly conclusive."

"Nothing's conclusive, Chief."

"You got any idea whose Social Security number this is?"

"Actually, I do."

"Really? How is that?"

"Something someone said."

"Now you got me interested. Who said what?"

"I'd rather not say."

"Why not?"

"I could be wrong."

"You could be wrong about who said what?"

"No. Just what it meant."

"You mean it might not be the number?"

"That's right."

It was.

The IRS agent called fifteen minutes later. His lawyer must have read him the riot act, because the man was rather chastened.

"I traced the number for you."

"Good."

"You will make note of the fact the IRS is cooperating fully with your investigation, and has done everything in its power to help?"

"Of course."

"On the other hand, you will remember that you officially requested this informa-

tion, and that it was not given out with reck-
less disregard, but only provided in the
course of a legal investigation, to which we
were compelled to comply?"

"You're a prince. Who is it?"

"A Mr. Hideki Takiyama."

CHAPTER 36

Hideki Takiyama was outraged. His face was red, making his scar even more pronounced. He drew back, tilted up his chin. "I do not understand."

"I"m sorry," Chief Harper said. "We need to ask you a few questions."

"Why?"

"Your name has come up in connection with the murder of this private investigator."

"My name?"

"Yes."

"How? I do not know this man. Do I need a lawyer?"

"Do you?"

"I do not know. Tell me, please, what you mean."

"Some of the clues point to you."

"Point?"

"If you would just come down to the station."

Chief Harper had found Hideki at his bed-and-breakfast. The Jacobsons seemed more than a little interested in their lodger's affairs. Having him questioned by Chief Harper with Cora in tow was almost too good to be true, unless it prevented him from paying his bill.

"I will come to the station because I wish to cooperate. But I do not understand."

In Hideki's case, coming down to the station meant walking a block and a half. During the trip he made a call on his cell phone. Chief Harper and Cora couldn't hear who he called, but Becky Baldwin met them at the police station door.

"You arrested my client?" Becky said.

"He's your client?"

"Yes, he is."

"I thought your client was Dennis Pride."

"He's also my client."

"That's a conflict of interest."

"Not at all. You arrested my client, Dennis Pride. You saw the error of your ways and let him go. He isn't charged with anything. He has nothing to do with this crime. So I'm perfectly free to represent Mr. Takiyama. Who also isn't charged with this crime." Becky raised her eyebrows at Chief Harper. "Is he?"

"We just want to talk to him."

"Is that the editorial *we*, the prosecutorial *we*, or you and Cora Felton? Who has very little legal standing."

"We just want to discuss the facts."

"I'd be glad to hear your version of them."

A crowd was gathering from among the people going in and out of Cushman's Bakeshop.

"Why don't we continue this inside," Harper said.

"Interrogation room, or office?" Becky asked as the chief ushered them in.

"Office," Harper said. "No one's taking anything down. This is just a casual conversation."

When they were all seated, Becky said, "All right. What are we talking about?"

"The second murder. Lester Mathews. Found stabbed with a samurai sword."

Becky grimaced. "Here I must point out the word *samurai* is certainly inflammatory. Seeing as how my client is Japanese."

"Funny you should mention it," Cora said.

Becky looked at her in surprise. "I beg your pardon?"

Chief Harper looked pained. "If I could do this my own way."

"Oh, phooey," Cora said. "Stop dragging it out. We're talking about something Aoki said about Hideki."

Hideki's eyes blazed. "*Aoki* said something about me?"

Becky frowned. "What are you talking about?"

"Hideki was born in the United States. Granted, he's lived most of his life in Japan. But, technically, that makes him an American citizen. That's what Aoki meant, wasn't it? As an American citizen, he has a Social Security number. His Social Security number is five-one-eight, three-two, seven-nine-four-six. Which is too bad."

"Why?"

Cora passed over the copy of the sudoku with the middle line circled. "This was found on the body."

Hideki was incensed. "I didn't do it!"

"No one is saying you did it."

"Yes, you are! You are saying the evidence says it was me."

"No, we're saying the evidence says it was your Social Security number. It doesn't mean you did it. It only means there's just an umpty-billion-to-one chance that this was a coincidence." Cora smiled. "You see why that's a problem."

"It's not a problem," Becky said. "If what you say is true —"

"You doubt our word?"

"No. I'm just being a lawyer and not

stipulating to anything that hasn't been proven. But, if that's the case, it means my client is being framed. It means someone went to a great deal of trouble to frame him. I certainly hope the police will bend every effort toward finding out who that might be."

"You think you are being framed, Mr. Taki-yama?"

"Of course I am being framed! Why would I write my own number? It is ridiculous!"

"Who would want to frame you?"

"Do you have to ask?"

"Oh," Harper said. "You think it should be obvious?"

"I am not making accusations," Hideki said. "I trust the police to do their job."

"I don't," Becky said. "No offense meant, but I'm not trusting anything. I want assurances that everything will be done, and I also want to see the results of that labor. If there are no results, I would like a damn good explanation of why there aren't."

"Easy there," Chief Harper said. "No one's trying to pull a fast one here. I ask the man who might be the person framing him. He doesn't want to tell me, that's fine. But then don't blame me for not knowing. It appears that Mr. Takiyama's Social Security number was used to connect him to a crime. Whether it was used by him or by some other person is open to discussion. I have heard an argument advanced why it wouldn't be him. I have not heard any argument advanced why it might be someone else. I know you wouldn't want to make a false accusation, and you're all falling all over each other to make sure that doesn't happen, but between you, me, and the lamppost, I would be far more inclined to pursue the prosecution of a third party if I were given some indication of who that third party might be."

"Your objection is noted," Becky said. "May I ask if my client is being charged with anything?"

"I'll have to check with the prosecutor."

"You do that." Becky smiled. "If you do it quickly enough, I won't charge you with false arrest."

CHAPTER 37

Cora found Sherry and Aaron at the *Baker-haven Gazette* and brought them up to date on the case.

"Becky Baldwin?" Aaron said. "She's his lawyer?"

"That's right."

"Isn't that a conflict of interest?"

"Apparently she needs the money."

"Hey, I gotta see about this."

Aaron grabbed his notebook, headed out the door.

"Thanks a lot," Sherry said.

"For what?"

"Sending him after Becky Baldwin. We were just having a nice talk."

"It can't be that nice. You hang out at your guy's office, it's never a good sign. It means the relationship's in trouble. In my case it was usually some secretary or other. That's not true here, but even so."

"What do you want?" Sherry said irritably.

"If you'd like to be happily married, you won't get there by talking things out at work."

"You dropped me off," Sherry pointed out.

"I wanted to get rid of you. I had business with the police."

"Well, thanks a lot."

"You needed to talk to Aaron. You talked to Aaron. Fine. Leave it at that. It's nearly noon. Whaddya say we catch some lunch?"

"I'm not in the mood."

"No, but you need to eat. Otherwise you'll get in the mood an hour from now, and there'll be nothing there."

Sherry and Cora walked down to the Wicker Basket, a popular home-style restaurant just off Main Street. Sherry ordered a salad. Cora had a burger and fries.

"You want bacon on that?" the waitress said.

"Knock me out," Cora told her.

"So, what's up?" Sherry asked. "Please tell me you don't have a puzzle for me to solve."

"Just the one we found in the safe."

"You said that was in the paper."

"Yeah. So?"

"I don't have to solve it. I wrote it. Let me see it, I'll tell you what it says."

"Chief Harper's got it."

"He's not bugging you for it?"

"He's a little busy at the moment."

Cora filled Sherry in.

"So, Hideki suspects someone of framing him, but he won't say who."

"Right," Cora says. "Which is transparent as all hell. Everyone knows he means Aoki. Which makes no sense."

"Why does it make no sense? They clearly hate each other. And Aoki aced Hideki out on your contract."

"I wouldn't wanna be accused of false modesty, but I doubt if I'm worth killing over. And I'm certainly not worth *framing* someone over."

"What's the difference?"

"Huge difference. You kill someone in the heat of passion. By passion I don't mean makin' whoopee. You get mad and you kill him. Wham, he's dead. To frame somebody, you plot, and plan, and go out of your way. Particularly to frame somebody in such a complicated fashion. Throw in a crossword puzzle *and* a sudoku? Give me a break! There's a very good chance the puzzle doesn't get solved and the frame doesn't work at all."

"With the Puzzle Lady on the scene?"

Cora grimaced. "That is, unfortunately,

the case. Put me in the mix and some moron thinks I'm capable of figuring out some complicated scheme. Maybe I am, but why go to all that trouble?"

"Payback, for stealing you away? But he *didn't* steal you away. You were stolen away from *him*."

Cora frowned. "That's right. Even if it was the other way around, what an unconvincing motive for laying such an elaborate trap. To snare your rival. Take delight in seeing the wheels of justice grind slowly, inexorably —" Cora broke off. "Do justice wheels grind?"

"Never mind. I get the point."

"The guys may get a kick out of screwing each other in a business deal. But this doesn't compute. There's just no passion involved."

Cora pointed to the door. "On the other hand, there's one very passionate woman."

Reiko came in, dressed in her geisha garb. She was mysteriously seductive, even more so than in her slinky sweater.

"There's a woman who, if she thought her husband was straying, might have the passion to act."

"You think Hideki's straying?"

"I have no idea. I don't know these people. They're from out of town. I don't know what's in their backgrounds that might lead to something like this. All I know is two private investigators have been hired, and they both wound up dead. That's not very promising. If I were a private investigator, I'd think twice before taking the case."

"You *are* a private investigator."

"Thanks a lot. If someone stabs me with a samurai sword, you're going to feel very guilty."

A waitress with menus approached Reiko. In a clear voice she said, "Two please. My husband is joining me." The waitress showed her to a table by the window.

"So, Hideki's coming," Cora observed. "That Becky Baldwin does work fast. One good thing. This murder charge should keep him too busy to worry about being dorked out of a sudoku book."

"Shh!" Sherry hissed.

"What?"

"Behind you."

Reiko swooped down on their table in a flurry of silk. It was disconcerting, particularly to someone who hadn't seen her coming.

"I am sorry," she said, noting Cora's expression. "I do not mean to intrude. But I need your help."

"My help?"

"Yes. I am afraid my husband is in trouble."

"I'm afraid you're right. But there's not much I can do."

"I want to hire you. To help him. Can you do that?"

"I don't know."

"But you can try?"

"Well . . ."

She opened her purse. "I will pay you. To help my husband."

"A private investigator usually works through a lawyer."

"I do not want a lawyer. I want you to work for me to prove my husband innocent of this horrible crime."

"It's somewhat unusual."

"I have money."

"Money always helps."

Reiko took out her wallet, counted out ten one-hundred-dollar bills. "Can you help me?"

Cora riffled through the bills, folded them up in her hand. "Yes, I can."

She heaved a sigh. "Oh. Thank you. Thank you. I am so relieved. I must go to my table now. Before he gets here."

"You don't want him to know you hired me?"

"It would not be honorable. He is very

proud. I can trust you, yes?"

Cora frowned. "This is most unusual."

"Oh! Here he comes!"

Reiko scurried back to her table.

And in walked Aoki.

CHAPTER 38

"It's my worst nightmare!" Cora wailed.

"Calm down."

"Not only did I get the wrong Asian man, but, by mixing them up, I got the one most likely to have committed the murder."

"It's not your fault," Sherry told her.

"That's no consolation. Nothing is my fault, but everything is wrong. Since the very beginning, every time I turn around I get the wrong Japanese man. It's not like I've mistaken them for each other. They don't *look* like each other. But I still keep mixing them up."

"You could have said no."

"I'd already said yes. What was I gonna do, say, 'Sorry, I thought you were talking about your *other* husband'?"

"That would have been a little awkward. Particularly since he wasn't supposed to know about it."

"No kidding. Can you think of any explanation I could have made that would not have been utterly humiliating?"

"No, I'll give you that."

"And, I got no real reason to turn down the job except for the fact the guy's probably guilty."

"You don't know that."

"Yes, I do. Everything points to it. The minute you realize *Aoki* is Geisha Girl's husband, it all falls into place. Hideki's messing around with his wife. The guy sets him up for revenge. Which takes care of my biggest problem. A passionless murder. You throw sex into the situation, the whole thing explodes."

"For the sake of argument, say you're right. It still has to make sense. Where did the private eye come in?"

"Aoki hires him. To keep tabs on his wife. The guy tells him his wife is indeed stepping out with his rival. Bad news for the private eye. Aoki never heard the phrase *don't shoot the messenger.* In a fit of rage, he stabs him with a samurai sword. He then proceeds to make it look like Hideki did."

"So he calmly sits down and writes out a sudoku based on Hideki's Social Security number. Then he constructs a crossword puzzle to tell you where to look for it. That seems pretty coolheaded for someone who's just committed murder. Not to mention ambitious."

"Don't be silly," Cora said. "The puzzles were created in advance. He was setting Hideki up, he just didn't know for what. Murder was the icing on the cake."

"And what about the first private eye?"

"What about him?"

"Where does he come in?"

"Same deal."

"Hired to watch Aoki's wife?"

"Why not?"

"And he didn't like the report, so he killed him and hired another one?" Sherry said ironically.

Cora grimaced. "I admit that does sound bad."

"So spell it out for me so it doesn't."

"I haven't worked all the kinks out."

"No kidding."

"But I don't have to buy the premise."

"What premise?"

"That Aoki hired both private eyes."

Sherry stared at her aunt. "Oh, you think that's better? That two separate people hired two separate eyes, both of whom wind up dead in Bakerhaven, Connecticut?"

"Just because something is totally illogical doesn't mean it didn't happen. What's more, it *did* happen. We're not in the position of adopting a smug, superior attitude and saying, 'Hey, that can't be true.' "

"I wasn't aware of being smug and superior."

"You're shooting down all my theories, and while your points are certainly valid, two men are still dead. So, how did they get that way?"

"I have no idea."

"I have no idea, either. Unlike you, I find myself in the position of being blamed for it."

"Unlike you, I wasn't hired to find out."

Cora shook her head. "You're good. Just when I think I'm winning the argument, you manage to trip me up."

"I'm not sure winning the argument is really the point."

"Like that," Cora said. "You're absolutely right. The point is figuring out what happened. Who the killer is, I don't know. But every idea I throw out you skewer. And rightfully so. They're stupid. It makes no sense if Aoki hired both private eyes. It makes no sense if two other people hired them. Now I gotta shut that out and say, if that's the case, illogical as it seems, how did it happen?"

"Isn't there something about if you eliminate the impossible, what's left, no matter how improbable, must be true?"

"Yeah. And it doesn't help. But that's where we are."

"What about the sword?"

"The murder weapon?"

"Uh-huh. If your theory is right, someone had to steal it from Dennis's car. Now how does that make sense? Along with these theories you're laying out for private eye dispatching."

"There are two ways it works. One, the murder weapon is opportunistic. Aoki, passing Dennis's car, sees the sword lying in the backseat, and can't resist stealing the sucker. Two, Dennis, confronted with the private eye, can't resist sticking the sword in his chest and inventing the story."

"Whoa," Sherry said. "No fair."

"You think Dennis couldn't do such a thing? Even drunk as a skunk?"

"I thought you established the sword was stolen from his car *before* the murder. I thought you found the broken window, confronted him with the receipt."

"I did."

"So?"

"So," Cora said, "Dennis can reason as well as anyone else. If he's stolen a sword to commit a murder, it would certainly behoove him to establish the murder weapon was out of his possession before the murder took place."

"So he smashes his window and gets it repaired just so he can claim the sword was stolen?"

"Why not?"

"That would imply premeditation."

"You don't think Dennis capable of premeditation?"

"A premeditated murder?"

"He stole the sword. Even he doesn't deny that. If he stole the sword, for whatever reason, he could pretend to have it stolen from him for the *same* reason. Or simply because he panicked when he realized he was in possession of the sword."

"That's assuming he's innocent. You were saying if he was guilty."

"Same thing. He finds he's stolen a sword. He pretends the sword's been stolen from him. It isn't. And, when confronted with a threat, he reacts."

"I thought you searched his car and the sword was gone."

"From his car, yes. He could have stashed it somewhere else."

"That's far-fetched."

Cora raised her finger. "Uh-uh. We're not allowing the far-fetched objection. *All* of this is far-fetched. What we're looking for is *pos-*

sible. He panicked about stealing the sword, smashed the window, had it repaired, ditched the sword somewhere so he could claim it was stolen. Where he ditched it is another matter. Knowing Dennis, I wouldn't be surprised if he put it in our silverware drawer."

"Cora!"

"You're right, he didn't. It's too big. And I seriously don't think he did anything. Except stealing the sword, which we know. The problem is, everything points to the fact Aoki did it. And he's my client. And he's *not* Becky Baldwin's client. She got the *right* Japanese publisher. By coincidence, you got the wrong one, too, so I got the one with our book contract. But that will be small consolation when they cart him off to jail. I doubt if he can publish it from there."

There came the sound of tires on gravel.

"Ah. Aaron must have finished his story. Now, you kids play nice. I'm tired of being cast in the role of the referee."

"Well, if you stop feeding him news stories . . ."

"Oh, now the killings are my fault. It's bad enough I haven't solved them, you're going to blame me for the fact they happened."

There came a knock on the door.

"It's not Aaron. You expecting anyone?"

Sherry shook her head.

Cora opened the front door.

Dennis Pride stood on the stoop. Compared to his recent court appearance, he was in pretty good shape, with his hair combed back and his tie tied.

That cut no ice with Cora. "You can't be here, Dennis. Go away, or I'll call the cops."

"I'm not here to see Sherry. I'm here to see you. You wanna come outside? We can maintain the legal limit."

"Fine."

Cora stepped outside, closed the door, led Dennis down the path. "I'm walking you back to your car. When we get there, you're getting in it and driving away. Anything you want to say to me, you better say between now and then."

"The night of the murder. It's coming back to me now. I'm remembering things."

"You remember the murder."

"Of course not. But I remember the night. I remember talking to you in the bar."

"You remember me showing you the receipt?"

"Yeah."

"Was that a surprise?"

"Sure. I don't know how you got in my car."

"You left it unlocked."

"Oh." Dennis put up his hands. "Look. I made a statement, the statement was true. I had the sword. It got stolen. I got the window repaired. That's all I have to say on the matter, and all Becky wants me to say. I'm talking about later."

"What about later?"

"When I left the bar. I didn't remember anything before. Now I do."

"What's that?"

"The Japanese guy. Who was drinking with Sherry. What's he all about?"

"He's a publisher. Wants to do a book of my sudoku."

"But you can't do them."

"No, actually I can. Sherry's good at words. I'm good at numbers."

The front door opened and Sherry came out.

"What are you talking about?"

"Go back in the house," Cora said.

"I want to know what's going on."

"What's going on is the police can't enforce a restraining order against this bozo if you're the one breaking it. Go back in the house, I'll get rid of him as soon as I can."

"Oh, hell," Sherry said. "Just get him out of here! Make him go!"

"He's telling me about the murder. He'll

253

go in a minute."

Aaron Grant's car rumbled up the drive-way.

"See!" Sherry said. "Now look what you've done!"

Aaron slammed his car to a stop, hopped out, bore down on Dennis.

"He's here to see me," Cora said. "Take Sherry out of range and I'll get rid of him."

Aaron flashed her an exasperated look, headed for the house. Sherry went in, closed the door. Aaron followed moments later.

"Okay," Cora said. "You got what you wanted. Disrupted their lives, caused another fight. Now, you want to tell me something, the clock is ticking. What you got?"

"I remember leaving the Country Kitchen. It's kind of foggy, but I remember driving away."

"Yeah? So what happened?"

"Nothing. Got lost and passed out."

"I know that. I thought you said you remembered something."

"I don't really remember. It's just a feeling."

"A feeling?"

"Yeah."

"What kind of feeling?"

"Like I was being followed."

CHAPTER 39

Cora picked the avocado out of Sherry's salad and savored every piece. "God, I love avocado."

No one noticed. Sherry was busy cooking, Aaron and Sherry were busy not attacking each other verbally (no small accomplishment, in Cora's opinion), and all three were busy watching the evening news.

On the small screen of the kitchen TV, Rick Reed was waxing eloquent. "Murder in Bakerhaven," he proclaimed. "Two unique but similar crimes." If that concept tripped him up, Rick didn't show it. "One might ask, how can that be?"

"I was just about to." Cora ate another piece of avocado.

"Well, the police believe the first body was dumped, since no murder weapon was found at the scene of the crime. But channel eight has it on good authority that a samurai sword figured in the second killing."

"That 'good authority' wouldn't happen to be my column, would it, Rick?" Aaron said sarcastically.

The newscast cut to a shot of Chief Harper. "No comment . . ."

Back on Rick. ". . . Was all Police Chief Dale Harper would say. But the police have picked up a suspect. No one is making any accusations and no charges have been filed, but the police are reported to have questioned Japanese publisher Hideki Takiyama. Mr. Takiyama had no statement, but he has hired hotshot Bakerhaven attorney Rebecca Baldwin to look out for his interests."

Becky Baldwin's face filled the screen. "This is a most unfortunate incident. My client is cooperating fully with the police, but he has little light to shed on the matter, as he knows absolutely nothing about it."

"And there you have it. The decedent, Lester Mathews, a New York private eye. What was he doing in Bakerhaven? And what did he stumble on that caused him to be killed? This is Rick Reed, channel eight news."

"Good lord," Cora said. "I just watched that news report and I know less than I did before."

"That's Rick's trademark," Aaron said. "Incredulous stupefaction. You wind up scratching your head thinking he couldn't really be that stupid, and you miss the whole newscast."

"There's nothing to miss because he doesn't have anything. He doesn't know about the Social Security number. And he's *alluding* to the arrest of the *wrong* Japanese publisher. Not even realizing there is a *right* Japanese publisher. No wonder he's so far off the mark."

"Not that far off the mark," Aaron said. "I know there's a right Japanese publisher, and I can't report it either."

"That's because it isn't news. What you know and I know is worthless. Until someone acts on it, it might as well not exist." Cora smacked her lips. "This is a great salad. What's in it?"

"There *was* avocado in it," Sherry said. "Until you picked it out."

"Well, you could have used more. That's the only complaint I have about the salad. Insufficient avocado."

"I used a whole avocado."

"It's gone."

"You ate a whole avocado?" Sherry looked in the salad bowl. "Oh, my God!"

"Shoot me. I told you we should have

eaten earlier."

"I told you we should have ordered out."

"This isn't New York."

"There's pizza."

"Girls, girls," Aaron said. "Talk about the dinner later. Right now I want to know more about the stuff I can't print."

"That's the spirit," Cora said. "See, Sherry, the guy's a prince. I'm sorry I have to withhold so much from him."

"Hey!" Aaron said. "What are you withholding?"

"Not a damn thing you can print. I just happen to have been retained in the case."

"Becky Baldwin hired you?"

"No, she didn't."

"Hideki hired you directly?"

"Not directly, no. Not indirectly, either, if that was your next question."

"Tell him," Sherry said. "You know he won't print it."

"Tell me what?"

Cora gave Aaron a rundown of her talk with Reiko.

Aaron was incredulous. "You're representing Aoki? But you haven't heard his story because his wife doesn't want you to talk to him?"

"That's it in a nutshell."

"I can see why this would be hard for me

to write."

"Yeah. Glad we're all on the same page."

Aaron tasted the stew on the stove. "Needs a little salt."

"Get out of there, you!"

Sherry started tickling him, and the two of them began roughhousing around the kitchen.

"I don't want to ruin the mood," Aaron said, "but can anyone tell me briefly what Dennis wanted this afternoon."

Sherry scowled.

"Moron," Cora said. "You don't want to ruin the mood, and then you drop the D-bomb. He was here because he trusts me to figure this out before the cops." She jerked her thumb at Sherry. "Aside from thinking she's pretty neat, it's probably the only bright idea the guy's ever had."

"But what did he want?"

"He just wanted me to know he remembered something about the night of the murder."

"Really? And what was that?"

"He thought he was being followed."

Aaron dropped his spoon. It clattered to the kitchen floor.

Sherry looked around accusingly. "I told you to stop tasting that."

"Sorry."

"It was just an impression," Cora said. "He was still pretty drunk."

"But you don't think he killed him?"

"No."

"Why?"

"Same reason you don't. He wouldn't have the nerve."

The TV came back from commercial.

"This is Rick Reed, with late-breaking news in the murder case of New York private detective, Lester Mathews. I am standing here in front of the Bakerhaven police station, where the police have just made an arrest. Details are sketchy, but we have it on good authority the suspect is not a local resident. I hope to have more on this story shortly —" Rick broke off, glanced to his left, reached out of frame. "I have just received confirmation on the identification of the suspect. The man under arrest is a Japanese publisher in town on business."

Rick paused for effect. He might have been announcing the Oscar winner. "Mr. Aoki Yoshiaki!"

CHAPTER 40

Cora Felton sized up the diminutive attorney. He looked like a kid playing dress up. His suit was two sizes too big for him, and he had a runny nose. "You're Aoki's lawyer?"

The little man snuffled. "That's right."

"You're a criminal attorney?"

"No."

"What's your specialty?"

"I'm an entertainment lawyer."

"You handle movie contracts?"

"And TV. And books."

"What do you know about criminal cases?"

"Not much."

"Don't you think Aoki should have a criminal attorney?"

"That's what I told him."

"What did he say?"

"He wants me."

"Why?" Cora waved her hand. "No offense meant."

"None taken. I wouldn't choose me, either. It may be a cultural thing: it would not be honorable not to use his attorney."

"Why don't you ask him if it is?"

"It might not be honorable to ask."

"Oh, for Christ's sake. Can I talk to him?"

"His wife employed you?"

"That's right."

"He didn't."

"She employed me to represent his interests."

"Now, that's a distinction I've come up against in the course of my entertainment career. It usually gets thrown out of court."

"This is not the same thing."

"No, but it could be. How do I know my client's interests and his wife's aren't opposed?"

"I give you my word."

"And you know this how?"

"I'm guessing."

The little attorney smiled. "You don't mince words, do you?"

"No. I've been hired to help the guy. If you don't want me to, that's fine. But it's a rather curious attitude. What have they got on your client?"

"They think he tried to frame his rival with a crossword puzzle and a sudoku."

"That's absurd."

"Tell me about it."

"That's not enough to hold him. What else have they got?"

"Fingerprints on a sword."

Cora's mouth fell open. "You're kidding."

"I'm not."

"Any sword in particular?"

"Seems it killed someone."

"You don't think Aoki needs a better lawyer?"

"That's what I've been trying to tell him."

"Let me."

It took a little doing, but a half hour later Cora found herself sitting across from Aoki in the interrogation room.

"This is ridiculous," Aoki declared. "I did not kill anyone."

"I'm glad to hear it. You mind telling me how you touched the sword."

"Yes, I do. My lawyer has told me not to talk."

"Your lawyer reviews book contracts. You want a legal opinion, get a criminal attorney."

"The only one in town is taken."

"Yes. By your rival. Ironic, isn't it. If you hadn't tried to frame him, you'd have had a lawyer to use."

"I didn't try to frame him."

"Someone did. Can you think of anyone with more motive than you?"

He rubbed his head. "This makes no sense."

"I agree. Unfortunately, that's not a plea that lets you out of jail. At the moment you got two people on your side. An entertainment lawyer, and me. Your choices are somewhat limited. You can let your lawyer sell your story as a TV movie of the week, or you can tell me what you know."

"You know what I know. It is a misunderstanding."

"Let's go back to you touching the sword."

"It was on my car."

"*On* your car?"

"You know. On the door. I open the door, it falls down."

"Outside your car?"

"Yes."

"It's leaning against the door of your car, you don't see it, you open the door, the sword falls to the ground?"

"Yes."

"So you pick it up. You see it's a samurai sword."

He raised a finger. "I do not think it is an authentic samurai sword. It is Japanese, but to qualify as a samurai —"

"Save it for *Antiques Roadshow.* What did

you *do* with it?"

"It was not mine. I leaned it up against the fence."

"What fence?"

"In the parking lot."

"What parking lot? This will go a lot faster if you realize I don't know what you know, and you fill me in."

"I am sorry. The restaurant parking lot. The Country Kitchen."

"What time was that?"

"It is afternoon. I have a late lunch."

Cora considered that. "Tell me about the private detective."

"I know nothing about the private detective."

"You didn't hire him?"

"No."

"You didn't hire a private eye to keep tabs on your wife?"

"Tabs?"

"To spy on your wife. To follow your wife. Your English is excellent. When you pretend you don't know what I mean, you're stalling. It makes me wonder why. Did you hire the private eye to follow your wife?"

"No."

"*Either* private eye?"

"Either?"

"There were two private eyes. Both wound

up dead."

"I understand."

"And you didn't hire either one?"

"No."

"And you didn't kill either one?"

"No."

"Did you meet either one?"

"No, I did not."

"Do you do sudoku?"

"What?"

"Sudoku puzzles. Can you do them?"

"Everyone can do them."

"Not everyone. Too bad you can."

"Why?"

"Tell me about Hideki."

Aoki's face clouded. "He is not a nice man."

"He's your rival."

"So?"

"You want to beat him."

"I would like my business to succeed. I would like him to stay out of it."

"And yet you came here to sign me to a contract."

"I think the book will sell."

"I certainly hope so. The point is, Hideki came here to sign me to a contract, so you came here to sign me to a contract."

"I was first."

"Oh?"

"It was my idea. Hideki came because I was here."

"Hideki spoke to me first."

"Uninvited? In a public place? Without an introduction? I called you at home."

"Which was the proper thing to do?"

"Of course."

"You went out and had drinks with my niece."

"Yes."

"You didn't tell her you were married."

"Why would that matter in a business deal?"

"You were having drinks. Where was your wife while you were having drinks with my niece?"

"She was at the room. How do you say, the bed-and-breakfast."

"Are you sure?"

"What do you mean?"

"She wasn't out with Hideki?"

"Of course not."

"How do you know?"

"Reiko would not do that."

"I'm pleased to hear it. Where were you born?"

"Born?"

"These aren't tough questions."

"I was born in Tokyo."

"So you're Japanese."

Aoki looked confused. "I do not understand."

"And Hideki isn't. Hideki was born in the United States. He's an American citizen."

"Is that important?"

"It was to you. You brought it up. In front of witnesses."

"Witnesses?"

"One witness in particular. Me. The person who could make the deduction."

"I do not understand."

Cora nodded. "That's probably a good line to take. I'm not sure how proficient entertainment lawyers are at murder strategy, but ignorance and bewilderment is most likely the way to play it."

He frowned. "I am not playing anything."

"Yes. And that's what I don't get. You hire the private eye to watch your wife. You prepare in advance the sudoku and the puzzle, to frame Hideki for the crime. Hideki, as you know he will, spots the private eye, confronts him, tells him to go to hell. At which point you step in, kill the unsuspecting gumshoe, and leave the clues that will lead me to Hideki. In all the confusion, you leave a fingerprint on the sword, ruining the perfect frame."

"You are wrong. My wife does not go near Hideki. I do not go near Hideki. Nothing you say is true."

"Nothing I say is true? Interesting. I say you hired the detective to follow your wife. If that isn't true, what is?" Cora studied him narrowly. "Suppose you hired the detective for another reason. Suppose you hired the detective to follow *Hideki.* If Hideki goes near your wife, the detective will report it. If Hideki doesn't go near your wife, the detective will report what he does. I like it. I like it much better. Hideki could catch the detective following him, and kill him with the sword. That would be good for you. Of course, it would mean admitting hiring the PI."

Aoki said nothing, stared straight ahead.

"On the other hand, it could be just as I said before. Hideki confronts the PI and roughs him up. Perhaps with some karate move that totally incapacitates him, but doesn't leave a mark. You come along and perform the coup de grâce. You like that better?"

Cora raised her arms over her head as if holding the hilt in both hands, then plunged an imaginary sword into the table with such force that Aoki slid backwards in his chair.

Aoki looked up at her, his eyes wide, his mouth open. "You are a very frightening woman."

Cora cocked her head.

"You ain't seen nothin' yet."

CHAPTER 41

Cora Felton smiled at Geisha Girl. "I'm going to need a few straight answers."

"Straight?"

"True. Correct. Not made up."

"I speak the truth."

"Good for you. You get a murder case, and people tend to hedge their bets. That's a gambling term, meaning —"

"I know what it means. I know English idiom."

"You spent time in this country?"

"A little."

"The same time as Hideki? You were his girlfriend?"

"No."

"No?"

"I was Aoki's girlfriend."

"Oh."

"We were in school together. Columbia University. In Manhattan. On the Upper West Side."

"Yeah, yeah. I'm from New York. Never mind the school. Tell me about the boys."

"I knew Aoki before. In Japan. He was proper. Respectful. Met my parents. Asked permission. Took me out."

"How romantic."

"You joke. Yes, it is, how do you say, old-fashioned? In America it is different. We are in college. On our own. We are free. We are young." Reiko smiled. "This is, of course, long ago."

"Of course." Cora managed a straight face. Geisha Girl couldn't be more than ten years out of college. "And you met Hideki?"

"Hideki is different. He is not proper. He is rude. Disrespectful. Wild. Even vulgar."

"So what happened?"

"Nothing happened."

"Give me a break. *Something* happened."

"He wanted me to go to a party. I said no. He would not listen. Aoki was angry."

"He asked you out in front of Aoki?"

"He was drinking. He was not respectful."

"Uh-huh. So what happened?"

"Hideki got into a terrible fight. Not with Aoki. At the party. Where I did not go."

"So you thought it was your fault?" Cora couldn't help sounding mocking.

"The hospital called me."

"The hospital?"

"Hideki gave them my name. At Emergency. When they asked him who to call."

"Son of a bitch."

"He was a mess. They sewed his face. He has the scar."

"A love token."

"After that, it is war. Aoki cannot stand Hideki. He does not want him around. But he wants to beat him. In everything, he must be better."

"You married Aoki."

"Of course. He was my intended."

"How did Hideki feel about that?"

"It is not his business."

"Right. So he quit trying, broke off the competition, and never bothered you again."

"He went back to Japan."

"And you stayed here?"

"We are back and forth. Sometimes here, sometimes there."

"Do you and Aoki always travel together?"

She raised her eyebrows. "What are you trying to imply."

"Give me a break. Your husband's on the hook for murder. I'm trying to be polite, but this is like pulling teeth. After your marriage, how did Hideki come back into your life?"

"He started a publishing house. Aoki was furious."

"Because he was also a publisher?"

"His father was a publisher. His father was very ill. When he died, Aoki inherited the company."

"What did Aoki do before?"

"Worked in the stock exchange. As an investor."

"He played the stock market with his father's money?"

Her face clouded. "That is not nice."

"Yeah, but you're not hiring me as a publicist. You're hiring me to keep hubby out of jail. From what I hear, that won't be easy."

"I do not understand."

"Well, your husband has every reason to hate Hideki. Hideki is an annoyance that can only be removed by drastic means. Killing him won't work because your husband will be the number-one suspect. But framing him — that's the way to go!" Cora shook her head. "Unfortunately, framing a man for murder is a high-risk game, and you don't get a second chance. One mistake and you're done. Like accidently leaving your fingerprint on a sword."

"Aoki explained that."

"Yeah. Exactly the type of clumsy explanation a careless killer would make up."

"My husband would not lie."

"Right, right, it would not be honorable." Cora waved it away. "Look, we got a little problem here. Hubby's on the hook, and he's got some bozo who reviews book contracts defending him. Honorable or not, we gotta get some help."

"How?"

"Leave it to me."

CHAPTER 42

"We should join forces," Cora said.

Becky's frown was skeptical. "Why?"

"We have clients with identical interests. Neither of them killed Lester Mathews, and we need to establish that point."

"We have clients with *conflicting* interests. I can prove my client didn't kill Lester Mathews by proving your client did."

"That seems a little harsh."

"Come on, Cora. Did you really expect me to fall for this?"

"Of course not. On the other hand, you're a lawyer, and I'm not."

"So what?"

"So what? Years of law school and you say, *So what?"*

"Stop kidding around. If you have a point, make it."

"You've been doing a good job of getting your clients out of jail. First Dennis. Then Hideki."

"So?"

"So, how'd you like to go for the hat trick?"

"I can't represent Aoki."

"Why not?"

"His interests are opposed to Hideki's."

"And Dennis's aren't?"

Becky frowned.

"You've already breached the conflict of interest barrier. Granted, with each client you take on, the odds that you are defending a guilty one dramatically increase. On the other hand, you're sure to get at least two out of three off."

"I'm glad you think it's funny."

"I don't think it's funny. I think it's awful. But I understand your not wanting to represent my client. You'd get a reputation for being easy."

"Watch it," Becky said.

"No offense meant. My reputation for being easy stood me in good stead right through college. Right though marriage, for that matter. You ever decide to take the plunge, I can give you hints."

"Could we stick to murder?"

"You bet. Here's the deal. You're not going to represent my client. I'm not going to work for yours. But we could pool a little information."

"Such as?" Becky asked.

"I wonder if your client mentioned spotting the deceased detective at any time."

"That's a rather major piece of information."

"I got a big one to trade."

"What's that?"

"How about my client saw the murder weapon?"

"I thought your client was picked up because his fingerprint was *on* the murder weapon."

"It could have got there any time. How about I pin it down?"

"You going to pin it down to the time and place of the murder?"

"What do you think?"

"I think you're going to admit that your client touched the sword on an occasion so far removed from the time and place of the murder you'd think it hardly mattered. I don't see that revelation as earth-shattering."

"I didn't think you would."

"Why are we really here?"

"I need a lawyer."

"Your client *has* a lawyer."

Cora sighed. "An entertainment lawyer. If the chief wanted to sign Aoki to a movie deal, he'd be just the man for the job."

"You think that's what Harper has in mind?"

"Somehow I tend to doubt it. Come on, Becky. Did Hideki tell you anything about this private eye? Anything at all?"

Becky sighed. "All right. I'm probably violating the canon of ethics and risking disbarment, but I'd like to get you out of my office, so I'm gonna cut you some slack and tell you exactly what my client told me about the private investigator."

"Really?" Cora said. "What?"

"Not a damn thing."

Chapter 43

Henry Firth looked more like a rat than ever. His nose twitched, his beady little eyes gleamed. "What are you trying to tell me?"

Cora Felton did her MC number. "Reiko is Aoki Yoshiaki's wife. She'd like him out of jail. She's retained my services to see that happens. Unfortunately, I'm not a lawyer, so you won't listen to me. Thats why I've hired Miss Rebecca Baldwin, attorney at law, to present our case for us."

"But . . . but . . . but . . ."

"Get a hold of yourself, Henry. You sound like a motorboat warming up."

"She can't represent him. She's representing Hideki Takiyama."

"And Dennis Pride," Cora reminded him. "Don't forget Dennis Pride."

"Exactly. You can't represent Aoki. It's a conflict of interest."

"Conflict of interest? With whom? Notice I said *whom,* so the grammar police won't throw me in jail."

"I'm glad you're having fun," Henry Firth said disapprovingly. "This happens to be murder."

"Really? Have you ruled out suicide?"

"Suicide?"

"Yes. Did Barney rule it out?"

"There was never a question of suicide."

"That's not true. The question of suicide has been raised."

"Who raised it?"

"I did. Just now. Weren't you listening?"

"Miss Felton —"

"Call me Cora."

The prosecutor went on as if he hadn't heard the interruption. "There is no question of suicide. The man was stabbed in the chest with a sword."

"But he's Japanese. They sometimes commit hari-kari as a matter of honor."

"Not this time. His fingers were cut to the bone trying to stop the blade."

"They were wrapped around it, weren't they?"

"Exactly."

"So if the guy tried to commit suicide, then changed his mind, and tried to push the sword out . . ."

Henry Firth shook his head. "We're not talking about suicide. We're talking about a cold-blooded, premeditated murder. In which one man went to great lengths to implicate another. It so happens we can prove it."

"How?" Cora asked.

"The sudoku and crossword puzzle implicate Mr. Yoshiaki."

"Really? Yesterday you said they implicated Mr. Takiyama."

"That was before we found Mr. Yoshiaki's fingerprint on the murder weapon."

"See, Becky," Cora said. "I told you that's all he had."

"All I have?" Henry Firth said ominously.

"He's basing his whole case on the one fingerprint. In light of it he's telling you what everything else means. A simple case of twisting the facts to fit the theory. I don't think you'll have much trouble proving him wrong."

"I don't think so either," Becky said. "I'm getting a writ of habeas corpus. Charge my client or release him."

"In that case, I'll charge him."

"Good," Cora said.

The prosecutor looked at her suspiciously. "Good?"

"Yeah." Cora smiled at him. "As long as you have someone charged with the crime, you won't be arresting anyone else."

CHAPTER 44

Cora Felton stretched out in a lawn chair in the backyard and blew smoke at the sky. "Ask me questions."

"What kind of questions?" Aaron said.

"Any questions. Anything at all."

"You must be desperate," Sherry said.

"Why?"

"To want our help."

"Did you ever have a crossword puzzle that didn't make sense? No, of course, you didn't. You write 'em. They mean what you want 'em to mean. Unless you're just a poor slob like me who has to solve 'em. Not that I ever do, but if I did. Anyway, that's the situation I'm in. I got all these facts, and they don't add up. Nothing *answers* all the questions. So I gotta make sure I've *asked* all the questions. I need someone to ask me questions to see if there's any I missed."

"Okay," Sherry said. "Who hired the detective?"

"Which detective?"

"The second one."

"Lester Mathews. Okay, you have two choices. Aoki hired the detective to watch his wife, and Hideki killed him. Aoki hired the detective to watch his wife in order to kill him to set up Hideki. The problem is, in either case Aoki hired the detective. Which he denies doing."

"He could be lying," Sherry said.

"Of course he could. But why would he lie to me? I'm on his side."

"You're on his side because you think he's innocent. If you thought he was guilty, it would be a different matter."

"If he told me he'd hired the private eye I'd think he was guilty?"

"Well, wouldn't you?"

"Of course I would. If he hired the private eye, it's either to watch his wife or frame Hideki, or both."

"How about he hires the private eye and Hideki kills him? It's simple, straight-forward, and —"

"And his fingerprint is on the sword," Cora finished for her. "That would be a fairly good indication he was involved. Even if it weren't for the elaborate attempt to frame Hideki with information only he knew."

"How do you know only he knew?"

"I don't." Cora turned to Aaron. "You're awfully quiet for a reporter. Don't you have any questions to kick in?"

"None I want to share."

Sherry looked at him. "What does *that* mean?"

"He thinks Dennis did it, and he doesn't want to say. That's it, isn't it?"

"Not that I think he did it," Aaron said. "It's just that we're taking his story at face value. Which I think is awfully generous."

"Granted," Cora said. "Except for the fact that none of us seriously suspect him. Any other questions?"

The phone rang in the house.

"I got it." Sherry went inside, poked her head out a moment later. "Chief Harper for you."

"It's about time. Maybe there's a break in the case."

Cora went in the kitchen to answer the phone. Buddy took it as an invitation to dart in and out of her legs in the most annoying fashion imaginable. Cora threw some kibble in his bowl, grabbed the receiver. "Hi, Chief. What's up?"

"The crossword puzzle we found in the detective's office."

"That's hardly news, Chief. I was there

285

when we found it."

"You never solved it."

"I don't *have* to solve it. It's not a clue. It's a stupid daily puzzle."

"I'd still like to know what it says."

"Why?"

"The guy had it in his safe."

"That's not my fault."

"I know it's not your fault. But it's your puzzle. And I want it solved. Can you come down here and fill it in?"

"I'm a little busy right now, Chief."

"Me too, what with this double homicide, and all. Which I understand you're messing into. Hiring Becky Baldwin, for God's sake."

"I didn't hire Becky Baldwin."

"Then what's she doing here?"

"His wife hired her."

"At your suggestion."

"Is that what she says?"

"That's what I say. Would you care to deny it?"

"You gonna charge me with soliciting business?"

"Is Becky giving you a kickback?"

"Would that be illegal? How about a commission?"

"You're not an agent. You're an investigator."

"Right. And if Becky wants to hire me to

investigate, that's hardly a kickback."

"Save it for the judge. Right now I want this puzzle solved."

"Fax it to me. Like you did the other one."

"That was different."

"Why?"

"It was a sheet of paper. It fit in the fax machine. This is a page in the newspaper."

"So scan it first."

"I hate scanning things."

"Me too. I have Sherry do it. Ask Dan."

Cora hung up the phone, went out in the backyard. "I'll be getting a fax. Chief Harper's sending me a puzzle."

"A sudoku?"

"No. A crossword."

"Wanna try solving it?" Sherry said.

"Why? Did hell freeze over?"

"Just a thought."

The fax came through five minutes later. Cora snatched it out of the machine. "Let's see. Ah, here's my smiling face. And it says: 'The Puzzle Lady has some advice on how to deal with an annoying, moody ex.' You remember that?"

"Vaguely," Sherry said. "I'll have to fill it in."

"Don't you have it in the computer?"

"I can probably solve it faster than I can find it."

"You need to upgrade your filing system."

"When do I ever have the time?"

"Good point."

Cora went back outside, where Aaron hadn't moved.

"Penny for your thoughts."

"Huh?"

"That clearly wasn't worth a penny. What's bugging you today?"

"Nothing."

"Listen, you're the Three M company, and I don't mean tape. You're moody, morose, and maudlin."

"Where the hell'd that come from?"

"Some husband or other. Just before I divorced him. I can't recall which one. I must have been in a funk."

"Yeah."

"Hey. You know Sherry comes with baggage. If you were smart, you'd lighten the load." Cora lit a cigarette, blew out the smoke. "Just a hint."

Sherry came out with the puzzle.

"Got it solved?"

"Yeah. You can fax it back to the chief."

"Is it going to help him?"

"How could it?"

"Good point. Let me see."

Cora took the crossword puzzle, read the long clues. " 'If he cries, and feels low, he

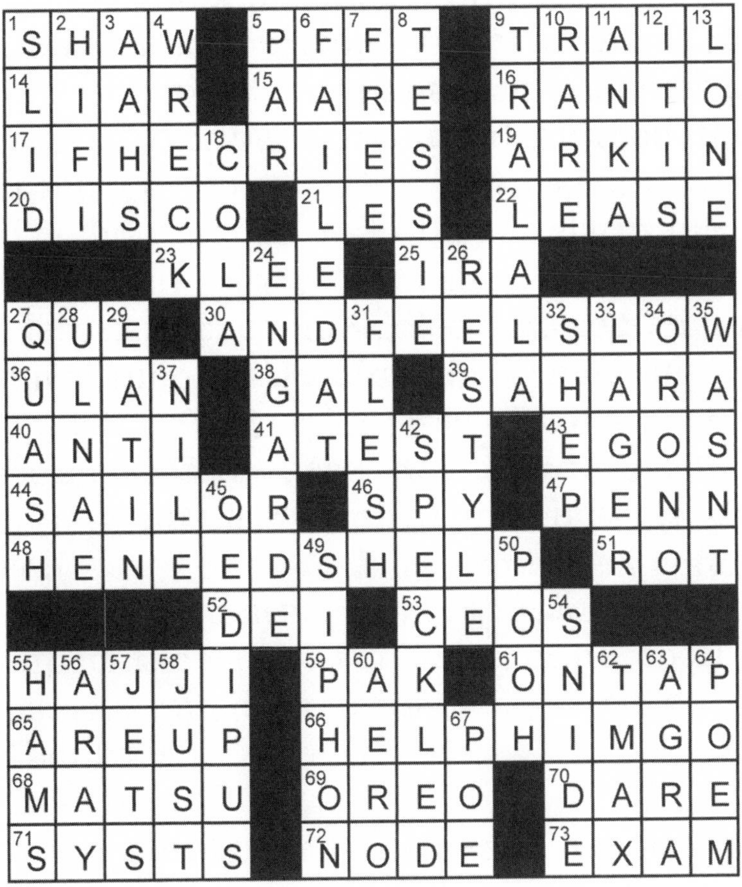
SHAW PFFT TRAIL
LIAR AARE RANTO
IFHECRIES ARKIN
DISCO LES LEASE
KLEE IRA
QUE ANDFEELSLOW
ULAN GAL SAHARA
ANTI ATEST EGOS
SAILOR SPY PENN
HENEEDSHELP ROT
DEI CEOS
HAJJI PAK ONTAP
AREUP HELPHIMGO
MATSU OREO DARE
SYSTS NODE EXAM

needs help, help him go.' " She frowned. "And that's the answer to how to deal with a moody, annoying ex?"

"It's as good as any."

"It's not great."

"Hey. I gotta come up with one of these every day of the week. Would you like to do it?"

Cora rolled her eyes. "Oh, hell, a crossword puzzle diva! No one's attacking your expertise. I'm just saying that answer is generic and meaningless."

"Thanks a bunch. *Generic and meaningless.* I'll be sure to blurb that on my résumé."

"In terms of the murder, silly. It has nothing to do with the murder."

"Of course it doesn't. How could it have anything to do with the murder?"

"It couldn't." Cora sighed. "Well, I guess I gotta take this to the chief. But it's not gonna help him at all."

CHAPTER 45

"This could be a clue," Chief Harper said.

Cora snorted. "Oh, for Christ's sake."

"It's about persistent lovers."

"And that's important because . . . ?"

"The Japanese triangle."

"I hope you didn't characterize it that way in the media."

"I haven't even alluded to it. But it's two guys fighting over a woman."

"She's married to one of them."

"Which makes it worse. The guys have a history. They hate each other's guts."

"Exactly."

"No, not exactly. One stinking poem about persistent ex-lovers has absolutely nothing to do with it."

"How do you know?"

"I'm not a moron. No offense meant, but what a stupid idea. A crossword puzzle in a newspaper has sinister connotations for real-life people?"

"Then why did the PI have it?"

"He had something wrapped in it. Like the money."

"The money wasn't wrapped in it."

"Are you sure?"

"I took the money out of the safe first. Then I took out the newspaper."

"Big deal."

"Folded open to this page."

"Yeah, but . . ."

"But what?"

Cora frowned, took her cigarettes out of her purse.

"Don't even think about it," Harper warned.

"But you want my help."

"No, I don't want your help. You're about to try to sell me on some damn fool idea of your own. You want to pitch it, fine, but you're pitching nicotine free."

"Steroids in baseball getting to you, Chief."

Harper sighed. "I like Hank Aaron."

"Who doesn't?" Cora pushed the cigarettes back in her purse. "Okay, here's the deal. You say clue, I say coincidence. Here's why. I'm the Puzzle Lady. You see a crossword puzzle, you think of me. Well, guess what. The world doesn't revolve around me. Or crossword puzzles, for that matter. A crossword in the paper doesn't mean a damn thing."

"I know. I'm just reacting to the moody-lover thing. This Japanese ménage à trois is a powder keg. I mean, they came here, ostensively to hire you. And they're *still* here. Granted, there's been a crime. Even so, I can't help feeling they're all running around playing emotional games with each other."

"When did they get here? Saturday?"

"I don't know. Why?"

"The first PI. Walter Krebb. Barney put the time of death at twenty-four to forty-eight hours before the body was found. So the guy was killed between Friday afternoon and Saturday afternoon. Most likely Friday night."

Harper picked up the phone. "Hey, Dan. Get Hideki's B and B on the phone, find out when he checked in. Call the Yoshiakis' B and B, ask 'em the same thing." After a pause, Harper said, " 'Cause I asked you to. I didn't say why." He hung up the phone. "Everyone wants you to justify yourself. You can't make a move without wondering if you're right."

"Dan's gonna do it?"

"Yeah. Not that it's gonna help. Like you say, they probably all checked in Saturday."

Dan called back ten minutes later. Harper

scooped up the phone. "Yeah? . . . Un-huh. . . . Un-huh . . . You're sure? . . . Okay, thanks, Dan." He hung up the phone. "Hideki checked in Saturday night."

"And?"

"Aoki checked in Saturday night."

"Told you so."

"Yes, you did."

"Then why aren't you happy?"

"Mrs. Yoshiaki didn't come with her husband. She checked in Friday afternoon."

CHAPTER 46

"Let's cut the crap."

Reiko clearly wasn't used to being talked to in this manner. She raised her eyebrows, glanced around the dining room. It was nearly empty. The Country Kitchen did light business at lunch. The hard-core drinkers were having burgers in the bar, didn't spill out into the dining room until happy hour.

"I beg your pardon."

Cora nodded. "Good English idiom. You've assimilated well."

"What are you talking about?"

"I'm talking about you and the boys. You've given me one story and it doesn't ring true. I was wondering if you'd like to try for two. Or is that the problem?"

Her face froze. "What?"

"Too convoluted? Let me be direct. Have you been playing these boys off against each other for fun and profit?"

"Fun and profit?"

"I just can't help myself. I will assume a language barrier. That's a generous assumption. That you're really baffled and not just feigning confusion to avoid answering the question."

Her eyes flicked.

"I see enough of that registered," Cora said. "You know what I'm talking about. So. You, Hideki, Aoki. What's the real story? Did you start with Aoki and go back to Aoki? Did you start with Hideki and wind up with Aoki? Have you been bouncing back and forth between the two since the dawn of time?"

"Dawn of time?"

Cora waggled her fingers. "Huh-uh. Not going to work anymore. You got the gist. Anything else is window dressing."

"Window dressing?"

"Now, stop that. Your husband is in jail. You want to get him out."

"Yes, of course."

"No, not of course. I've had husbands I'd have *left* in jail. Damn near all of them, now that I think of it. Why'd you come here early?"

"Early?"

"I'll give you that one. I threw the change of subject at you. To Bakerhaven. You came here before your husband. Why?"

"To rent the room."

"Come on. You could do that on the phone."

"To see that everything was all right."

"Why wouldn't it be?"

"My husband is a precise man. He likes everything just so."

"And if it hadn't been?"

"I would have refused to take the room."

"For that you came a whole day early?"

"Yes."

"Why? Why couldn't you change the room the next day if it was unsuitable?"

"Aoki wouldn't do that."

"Why?"

"It would not be honorable."

"But stealing another man's woman is?"

Her mouth fell open. "You are impertinent."

"I didn't mean you. I meant me. Your husband stole me away from Hideki."

"That's not true."

"Yes, it is. I've got a signed contract to prove it."

"You don't belong to Hideki. My husband had just as much right —"

Cora put up her hand. "Never mind. I don't care. You came here to rent a room?"

"Yes."

"And Hideki was not here?"

"No. Why would he be?"

"To see you."

"Hideki would not do that."

"Why? Because it wouldn't be honorable?"

"You are mocking me?"

"A little. Why don't you come off your high horse and tell me what's going on?"

"My high horse?"

"You're either very dense or very bright. I can't tell which. Most men don't care. Not when you look like you do. Have they always fought over you? Ever since this all began?"

"They do not fight over me."

"Yeah." Cora sighed. "Okay, that's about it."

"Can you help my husband?"

"I'll give it my best shot." Cora frowned, considered. "Can you tell me one more thing?"

"What's that?"

"Who cuts your hair?"

CHAPTER 47

The trendy salon on East Eighty-sixth Street was the type Cora only would have walked into with a gun to her head. The stylist working in the window had blond spikes in haphazard directions, and a stud in her nose. With pointy scissors she was attacking the head of a thirtysomething brunette woman who clearly needed a dramatic statement to take away from too much nose and chin. Whatever the stylist was going for Cora had no idea, but she was sure it would be ultramodern and costly.

Cora went in the shop, discovered there were three more stylists working within. A young woman with her hair knotted incongruously around a stubby pencil said, "May I help you?"

"I'll like to get my hair cut."

"Do you have an appointment?"

"No. I was told to ask for Mitzi. Is she free?"

Free did not describe it. Mitzi cost as much as a high-priced call girl. She had a physique like a soda straw, short-clipped hair, and a squeaky voice. She could have been a boy named Mitzi, assuming he was a castrato.

After a brief plea bargain ("Just a trim." "Leave it to me."), Mitzi snatched up her scissors, and Cora plunged into the task at hand.

Luckily, Mitzi helped her.

"You asked for me?"

"You were recommended."

"By who?"

Cora almost said, "By whom." She caught herself, said, "By Reiko."

"She recommended me? How sweet."

"Have you been cutting her hair long?"

"A couple of years."

"Oh? She's in New York that much?"

"They're back and forth."

"They?"

"She and her husband."

"Oh, him."

"Yeah. Him."

"Have they been getting along?"

"Why do you say that?"

"The way you said, 'Him.' " Cora winked at the woman. "I've been married a few times myself, so I know."

"Do you, now?" Mitzi frowned. "You look familiar. Have you been in here before?"

"First time."

"You sure?"

"I'd remember."

"I got the feeling I — Oh, my God! You're the Puzzle Lady!"

"Shhh! I'm incognito."

"You used to do those breakfast cereal commercials."

"Don't remind me."

"Wow, this is exciting. Not that we don't get famous people. Cindy had Jennifer Aniston once. Before the breakup."

Cora didn't ask which breakup, tried to steer the conversation gently back on point. "She never had marital problems, did she?"

"Who?"

"Reiko."

"Of course, I wouldn't talk about that," Mitzi said, and proceeded to do so.

In the next fifteen minutes Cora learned everything there was to know about the Japanese triangle.

It existed, all right. Reiko might deny it to Cora. Or to the police. But not to her hairdresser.

The men were mortal enemies, head over heels in love. Not that she led them on. But how could she help it? After the elaborate plans they laid. Hideki luring her husband to Boston for a bogus meeting with Stephen King. Her husband deliberately ensnaring Hideki in a lawsuit to frustrate the publication of an anthology of short stories. Hideki bribing the driver of Aoki's car service to get stuck in rush hour traffic. On and on and on. An endless tale of love and deceit.

But nothing on murder.

Nothing of violence.

Nothing suggesting a crime.

"Do you think her husband knows?" Cora asked.

"He has to. The way things are."

"Did she ever say he did?"

"She never said so, no."

"Is it possible he knows, but doesn't let on?"

Mitzi laughed. "Aoki? No way!"

"Why do you say that?"

"He's got a *temper.*" Mitzi rolled her eyes. "He looks *so* polite and mild-mannered, but, if things aren't perfect, believe me, he lets her know."

"Really?" Cora pursed her lips. "Has she ever come in bruised?"

"Bruised?"

"You know what I mean. Did he ever hurt her?"

Mitzi's smile was enormous. "Hurt *her?*

You gotta be kidding."

"What do you mean?"

"That's why she gets her hair cut here. It's in the neighborhood."

Cora frowned. "Neighborhood of what?"

"Her jujitsu class." Mitzi chuckled. "Reiko isn't exactly helpless. She's a fourth-degree black belt."

CHAPTER 48

Kyoto Martial Arts was a second-story walk-up over a flower shop on Lexington Avenue. A dozen youngsters ranging in age from eight to eighteen were being tutored in the fine art of flinging each other in all directions by an aging blond beach boy in a white uniform with a black belt. The children wore white uniforms with belts of various colors such as white, green, brown, and even one black. The black belt was worn by a skinny kid who couldn't have been more than twelve. When his turn came, he walked forward, bowed to an older, stockier kid in a green belt, and proceeded to toss him over his shoulder as if he were a sack of meal. One of the young mothers sitting at the side of the room beamed. Another looked horrified.

Cora waited until the class was over to approach the beach boy. Bad move. She was cut off by the mothers, who mobbed him while their kids were getting changed. At the same time, more kids were coming in and heading for the locker room, to change for the next class.

Cora squeezed in amongst the young mothers, flashed her most winning smile. "Excuse me. I'd like to talk to you about a class."

The beach boy tore himself away from an obviously smitten thirtysomething mother, looked at Cora, and did a double take. "For your grandson?" he inquired.

Cora didn't kill him, which she thought showed admirable restraint. "No. I want to talk to you about a class you teach."

He was trying not to stare, like he'd never seen a slightly older person before. "I don't understand."

Of course you don't, you mindless twit, hovered on the tip of Cora's tongue. She bit it back, said, "It's about one of your students. I need to know how much she knows."

He frowned. "I beg your pardon?"

"The kids have different colored belts. That means they passed different levels, right?"

"Of course."

"Does that reflect a degree of skill, or just the fact they paid to take the course?"

"Now, look here."

"No offense meant. But I need to know what your students are capable of. There's a young woman name Reiko. Is she one of your students?"

"Why?"

"I'm interested in her expertise. If she were attacked, would she be able to defend herself?"

He looked insulted. "Of course."

"Even against someone stronger? She would know techniques that would let her win?"

"I would put her up against someone who didn't know jujitsu any day of the week."

"What about weapons? Is she familiar with weapons? And how to use them?"

"Sure."

"A samurai sword, for instance. Could she kill someone with a samurai sword?"

He laughed.

"You find that funny?"

"She wouldn't *need* a samurai sword." The beach boy practically smirked. "Reiko could kill someone who *had* a samurai sword."

CHAPTER 49

"My God! What happened to you?" Sherry exclaimed.

Cora frowned. "What do you mean?"

"Are you kidding? You have teased hair, auburn highlights, and a sheepdog shag. You look like the retro aunt from hell."

"Oh, come on."

"How much did you pay?"

"A hundred and twenty bucks."

"I could have you committed. I could get you declared non compos mentis on that haircut alone."

"It can't be that bad."

Cora went in the bathroom.

Moments later, Sherry heard a shriek.

Cora stumbled out. "Oh! My! God!"

"Didn't you look at yourself in the beauty parlor?"

"No wonder I freaked out the beach boy."

"Beach boy?"

"Don't start that. You're not Japanese."

"What?"

"Everything's coming apart at the seams. This stupid case that doesn't make any sense. I start to follow the leads, and they're all in the wrong direction."

"What do you mean?"

Cora filled Sherry in on her conversations with Reiko and Mitzi.

"So what's the problem?"

"Reiko's lying. Which, of course, she would be, if she's a two-timing tramp. She's the one person in the scenario ruthless enough to kill. Her hands are lethal weapons."

"The guy was stabbed by a sword."

"A samurai sword. Which, if she's a fourth-degree black belt, she knows how to wield."

"So maybe she's guilty."

"Bite your tongue!"

"What's so bad about that?"

"Are you kidding? She's paying the bills. I can't unearth the evidence that hangs her, and then charge her for it."

"That's very ethical of you."

"You're in a good mood. You and Aaron patch things up?"

"Not so you could notice. He went off to the paper to work on the story."

"Just a hint. You might want to cut him some slack. Can you really blame him for reacting to Dennis?"

"I told him to ignore him."

"That's like ignoring the Ebola virus." Cora slumped down on the couch, rubbed her head. "What a mess." Her hand touched her hair. "Oh, God! It's shellacked down! I'll have to comb it with a blow-torch!"

"Just wear a hat."

"There's no hat big enough. My hair will stick out. I'll have to get one of those Rasta-farian caps to hide my dreadlocks."

"Dreadlocks would be an improvement."

Cora suggested diversions for her niece that would be illegal in most states.

Sherry ignored the jibe, said, "What about this woman? Do you really think she did it?"

"No. That doesn't mean the police won't."

Sherry grinned. "That would be a little embarrassing. If they charge her, would they have to let her husband out of jail?"

"Unless they can prove conspiracy."

"Can they?"

"Of course not. Neither of them is guilty."

"How do you know that?"

"Because they're paying the bills."

"I'm getting a headache," Sherry said.

"You should talk. You still got your own hair."

"Suppose that happened," Sherry said.

"They let her husband out and charged her, I mean."

"Yeah?"

"Could Becky represent her?"

Cora smiled for the first time since she looked in the mirror. "Wouldn't that be delicious. One murder, and Becky gets four fees out of it."

"Actually, there were *two* murders," Sherry said.

"Right. I mustn't forget that. Even though the first one seems so detached."

"Why is that?"

"Well, no car and no murder weapon. Granted, it's a New York PI, but there the similarities end."

"You think it's just coincidence?"

"That would be a pretty big coincidence. It's almost gotta be the same person, and that's what makes it bad for Geisha Girl."

"What do you mean?"

"She was here when it happened. The boys weren't. At least, in theory."

"You think they were?"

"I bet Hideki was. Aoki's wife was up here alone, don't you think he'd take a shot?"

"But he hadn't checked in yet."

"No. He'd have been commuting. Which would explain the presence of the private eye."

"You mean he followed him here from New York? And then Hideki killed him?"

"Or Geisha Girl killed him. Or someone else entirely."

"Like who?"

"Like Aoki."

"You think he did?"

"Absolutely not, since he's my client. But I can't rule him out."

"Why not?"

"Well, for one thing, there's fairly good evidence he framed Hideki for the other murder. If that's true, he's most likely guilty of this one."

"How does that make sense?"

"It doesn't. But none of this makes sense. It's all an ethereal Noh drama acted out by the spirits of the dead."

"You can't even justify the theory?"

"What theory?"

"That Aoki killed the first PI?"

"Sure I can. He hired him to watch his wife and Hideki. He drove up here with the PI to be on hand in case they hooked up. Hideki did, but the PI blew the surveillance and lost him. In a fit of rage, Aoki killed the PI. He drove the PI's car to Manhattan because he was stranded in Bakerhaven with no other way to get back."

Sherry's eyes widened. "That's not bad."

"It's not good, either. If he drove the PI's car back to Manhattan, the cops would have found it by now. But forget the first murder. If Aoki's the killer, then he tried to frame Hideki for the second murder. Which is ten times worse. You have to figure he hired a PI, got him out here just to kill him. Meanwhile constructed a crossword and sudoku that would implicate Hideki. Only they *don't* implicate Hideki because why would Hideki kill the man and then leave clues that prove he did it?"

"Arrogance," Sherry suggested.

"What?"

"The man is so arrogant he signs his crime, taunting his accusers. Daring them to figure it out."

"It's a theory." Cora grimaced. "It's a *bad* theory, but it's a theory."

CHAPTER 50

"Why are you wearing that hat?"

"I like this hat."

"It's too big for you."

"It's just right."

Cora had managed to hide her hair under a ten-gallon Stetson, a keepsake from her fourth husband, Henry, the fancied cowboy and poker player. He hadn't been much of either, but he had managed to corral a young filly from El Paso, whose name featured prominently as a corespondent in Cora's subsequent divorce complaint. Cora had gotten the house, the horse, and the hat. It occurred to her at the time she only needed Henry's hide to make her eligible for the 4-H Club.

"A cowboy hat?" Harper was grinning.

"Could we talk about something other than my headgear, Chief?"

"What did you have in mind?"

"I've been thinking about your prisoner."

"Me, too. Tomorrow I gotta charge him or let him go. Nobody's gonna be happy if I don't charge him. On the other hand, what have I got? There's more evidence against the other guy than there is against him."

"I understand. That's because he framed the other guy. Or, at least, that's the theory."

"I know that's the theory. But I really don't like it." He put up his hand. "Don't quote me on that, will you?"

"Not unless you charge *me* with the crime," Cora assured him. "Which is not entirely unlikely. You've charged everyone else."

"You know it's not my doing. I'm just following the facts."

"And Ratface's orders."

"True. He's the one who has to charge him or release him. Only, if he releases him, I'm the one who has to make another arrest."

"Aren't you running out of suspects?"

"Absolutely not. This isn't one of those mystery books you read. The killer doesn't have to be anyone you know. It could be someone from New York we never heard of."

"Who coincidently winds up in Bakerhaven just in time to commit two unrelated crimes."

"I'm not saying these are good theories.

But we don't have all the facts yet."

"Well, why don't we?" Cora said, irritably. "We've got two private eyes involved. Why isn't there any record of anyone hiring either one?"

"Are you implying there is and we just haven't found it?"

"I'm not *implying* that. It's the obvious conclusion."

"Hey, no fair. You searched that one PI's office yourself."

"Yeah, looking for a safe. We didn't take the place apart. We didn't search the guy's computer."

"But the New York cops did. The guy's Quicken account didn't show any recent deposit that might have come from a client. That, coupled with the cash in the safe, suggests he was paid in person."

"Then the client should have had an appointment," Cora insisted. "There should be something in the appointment book. A name. A time. A phone number. Or a message on the answering machine."

"There wasn't."

"So the client was a walk-in," Cora mused. "Either knew about him, or picked his name out of the phone book."

"Or just happened to be in the neighborhood," Harper said. "What was his office near?"

Cora frowned.

Walter Krebb's office wasn't near anything in particular.

But Lester Mathews's office was only a few blocks away from the beauty salon where Mitzi had worked such wonders on her hair.

CHAPTER 51

Cora found Aoki and his wife lunching at the Country Kitchen. Aoki was clearly fond of the salad bar, had a plate piled high.

Cora walked up to the table, bowed. "Sorry to bother you. I need to talk to your wife alone."

"That is not proper," Aoki said. His eyes were on her Stetson hat. Cora wasn't sure if he was referring to her headgear or her stated intention.

"I'm not going to suggest anything improper. I just have to ask a few questions."

"You can ask me."

"No, you're a murder suspect. Your lawyer wouldn't like it. Let me ask your wife. No one's charged her with anything yet."

Cora practically dragged Reiko away from the table. "Guess where I was."

Reiko frowned. "Where?"

"At the dojo."

"The what?"

"Isn't that what they call your jujitsu class?"

"No."

"What do you call it?"

"Jujitsu class."

"Fine. I talked to your teacher."

"Kiosh?"

"Guy looks like he should be riding a surfboard."

"Yes. He is not Japanese, but he is good."

"I'm glad to hear it. Do you know what he said?"

"I do not know what you are saying. But you make my husband mad."

"Sorry about that." Cora steered Reiko over to the salad bar, began munching on a carrot stick. "This won't take a moment. Your jujitsu class is very near something else."

"Yes. The beauty parlor."

"Guess again."

"But it is."

"I know it is. It's also near something else. Can you imagine what?"

"No. I cannot."

"I'll give you a hint. It has a magnifying glass, and it looks for clues."

Reiko frowned. "You are talking in a strange manner."

"The more frustrated I get, the more that

happens. I'm talking about a PI. A private investigator. A detective. A gumshoe. A private eye."

Reiko glanced back at the table. "My husband will be coming over."

"Good. Then you can tell him if you hired this detective."

"If I hired?"

"Oh, hell. Now we're back to repeating."

"I do not understand."

"There's nothing to understand. I'm asking if you hired the detective. It's a yes or no question. 'Yes' would imply that you did. 'No' would imply that you didn't. Care to choose one?"

"You are crazy. I cannot talk to you."

Rieko started back to her table.

Cora grabbed her by the arm. She fully expected to be flipped head over heels into the salad bar, but the woman merely stopped.

"Please," Reiko pleaded.

Cora looked her right in the eyes. "Did you hire the detective?"

There was a moment's hesitation. Cora could imagine the woman's rigid, extended fingers plunging into her stomach, yanking out her spine.

"No."

Reiko wrenched her hand away, walked

back to the table, just as her husband was preparing to get up.

Cora picked another carrot from the salad bar, chomped on it thoughtfully.

Reiko had been quite firm in her denial.

Cora wondered if she believed her.

CHAPTER 52

As Cora neared the police station, a young girl came out.

Cora winced at the thought. The *young girl* was probably in her late twenties, and she'd take offense at the appellation. Not that Cora gave a damn. Cora was just dismayed to realize that someone that age seemed young.

The you're-older-than-sin-reminder hesitated in the doorway before going down the steps. Seemed to be weighing a decision. If it was whether or not to have a cigarette, the answer was yes, because she pulled out a pack and lit one up.

Cora's immediate reaction was that she shouldn't be smoking. The girl, that is. Cora was a nicotine-addicted old dear who couldn't help herself. But the girl should know better.

Cora wondered if the girl was holding the door for her. Ordinarily, that would have been a nice gesture. But having just been mistaken for someone's grandmother, Cora saw it only as in deference to a dotty old lady in a cowboy hat. It was almost gratifying when the girl released the door and let it slam in her face.

But then why had the girl hesitated?

Cora found Chief Harper at his desk. "What did she want?"

"Who?"

"Girl was just here."

"Mary Dobbs?"

"If that's her name."

"Only young woman's been in today."

"What'd she want."

Harper frowned. "Well, aren't you the old busybody."

"Old?"

"I just mean who cares what some girl wants with everything else that's going on."

"You mean her visit had nothing to do with it?"

"No. Why would it?"

"I don't know. A young woman doesn't usually come down to the police station unless it's something important."

"She came to report a yowling cat."

"What?"

"Some cat keeping her up. She didn't know who it belonged to. I told her there wasn't much we could do. Call the next time it was yowling, and I'd send someone by."

"That's all she came for?"

"It may not sound like much. But if she wasn't getting any sleep . . ." Harper shrugged.

"She know anything about the crime?"

"No."

"You sure?"

"Sure, I'm sure."

"How do you know?"

"I asked her."

"Why would you ask her?"

"She works at the Country Kitchen."

"Really."

"Yeah. I thought she might have seen the detective leave. But she didn't."

"Was she on that night?"

"Yes, but she was working the dining room, didn't see who was in the bar. Why?"

"She looked nervous."

"How could you tell?"

"She came out the front door, lit a cigarette."

Harper snorted. "By that criterion, you're the most nervous person in town. So what have you got for me?"

"Oh. Reiko claims she didn't hire the PI."

"What?"

Cora filled the chief in on her conversation with Mrs. Yoshiaki.

Harper was incredulous. "You went up and asked her?"

"Yeah. I figured hinting wasn't going to do it."

"Damn it."

"It doesn't mean *you* can't ask her."

"Yeah. Now that you warned her."

"I'm not sure it matters, Chief. I mean, 'Did you hire a PI?' is a question a person who hired one would be apt to expect."

"That's not the point."

"I know it's not the point. The point is whether or not she carved the guy up. According to her jujitsu teacher, she wouldn't need a sword. Which doesn't mean she didn't use one."

"Maybe I should pull her in."

"On what charge."

"No charge. Just to ask her some questions."

"Small problem, Chief. Her husband is your current suspect. A wife can't testify against her husband, in case you forgot. You can ask all you want, but she doesn't have to answer."

"Damn." Harper scowled, considered. "You wanna bring me something I can use, for a change?"

Cora sighed. "Would I ever."

CHAPTER 53

"Do you have a cat?"

Mrs. Grayson's smile was forced. "Excuse me?"

"I'm sorry to bother you," Cora said, in her most placating voice. She had showered, shampooed her hair four times, and put on her Sunday-go-to-meetin' togs, in an effort to appear convivial. "I just wanted to know if you have a cat."

"Well, I don't."

"It won't get you in trouble," Cora assured her.

Mrs. Grayson's eyes narrowed. "I'm not lying."

"I'm not saying you are. I just want to be perfectly clear I'm not trying to make trouble."

"What are you trying to do?"

"I'm looking for a cat."

"I haven't got one."

"Too bad."

"Why?"

"I'm taking a survey. Making a list. For a *cat*alogue."

Mrs. Grayson never cracked a smile. "Haven't got one," she said, and closed the door.

Mrs. Murphy, two houses down, was far more gracious. "Do come in. Can I get you some tea?"

Cora knew the woman vaguely, had seen her in the bakery and the Wicker Basket, usually in the company of other chatty women. Cora tended to avoid chatty women.

"I really haven't time for tea."

Mrs. Murphy's eyes twinkled. "Perhaps a drop of brandy?"

"No," Cora said, slightly more sharply than the situation required. A drop of brandy was indeed an appealing offer, were she not on the wagon. "I'm awfully busy. I just have a couple of questions."

"About the murders?" Mrs. Murphy's eyes sparkled. "Isn't it *awful?* I understand you were there."

"I was there. I'm trying to clear up some of the details the police neglected. I was hoping you could help me out."

"You mean you actually saw the *body?*"

"Yes."

Mrs. Murphy shuddered deliciously. "That must have been *dreadful!* And now you need my help?"

"Yes."

"What do you need to know?"

"Do you have a cat?"

By the time Cora reached Mrs. Wickem, word had got around. "You've been calling on my neighbors."

"You saw me?"

"How could I miss? You parked in front of my house. But you don't come see me. You go next door. Talking to everyone. Why did you skip me?"

"Skip you?"

"You talked to Mrs. Grayson. You went right by me and talked to Mrs. Murphy."

"Just saving the best for last."

"I beg your pardon?"

"You don't have a cat, do you?"

"No. Why do you ask?"

"No reason. Is your boarder here?"

"Mary Dobbs? I think so."

"I need to talk to her."

Mary didn't seem pleased to see Cora. "What do you want?"

"Chief Harper sent me."

"Huh?"

"You went to see Chief Harper. About a cat."

"So?"

"He's been busy. With these murders, and all. He sent me to investigate."

"He sent you?"

"Yes. To investigate your complaint about a cat. I talked to the neighbors and they deny it. Which is not surprising. No one wants to admit complicity. You accuse someone of a crime, the first instinct is to deny. For instance, if I accused you of something, you wouldn't tell me, would you?"

"What do you mean?"

"You're a very lucky girl. Extremely lucky. Most girls don't get a second chance. They make a mistake and they're done." Cora frowned. "Often on homecoming week. But that's another story. The point is, there are crimes you're probably not aware of. You think of crime, you think robbery, murder, possession of drugs. There's also withholding evidence, obstruction of justice, perjury, and swearing out a false complaint."

"I don't know what you mean."

"Yes, you do. You're stalling. Hoping this isn't what you think it is. Bad news. It *is*." Cora smiled. "So tell me about the yowling cat."

CHAPTER 54

Chief Harper was apoplectic. "She *what?!*"

"Now, now, now," Cora said. "Don't be too hard on the girl. You're a very intimidating figure. No wonder she got scared."

"See here —"

Cora put up her hand. "No harm, no foul. The girl's come clean. Why not let it go?"

"Because you promised her I would?"

"I may have said something along those lines."

"Oh, for God's sake!"

"What, you want to prosecute her just because you can't get your killer? That's not going to play well, Chief. Even Rick Reed will make you look bad."

"People think they can come in here and lie to the police."

"At least she came," Cora pointed out. "Maybe she got cold feet, but at least she showed up. Anyway, now she's come clean, and we take it from there."

"From where?"

"From the report that she came here to make. She slipped out the back door to have a cigarette. Because there's no smoking in the Country Kitchen. When you talk about local ordinances that need an overhaul —"

"Cora."

"She was out in the parking lot, and she saw them leave."

"Who?"

"A Japanese man and woman."

"Could you be more specific."

"Well, it was dark, and —"

"Goddamn it!"

Cora raised her finger. "You see, Chief? That's why the girl lied. She started to tell her story and realized she was going to get that reaction. So she went with the yowling cat. Hmm."

"What?"

"Sounds like a Perry Mason title. The Case of the Yowling Cat."

"Yeah, great. This Asian couple. I take it that would be Mrs. Yoshiaki and a man who could have been her husband or could have been her lover?"

"Right. Moments later a second Asian man comes out."

"Who she couldn't identify, but who also could have been Hideki or Aoki?" Harper said disgustedly.

"Yeah, but we know the order they left the bar. Reiko ran out and Hideki followed. Aoki had a tussle with Dennis that slowed him down. So Aoki was the second man out. He ran up to the couple and they had a huge fight. Then the woman drove off with the man. The other man left alone."

"The same man who came out alone?"

"She's not sure."

"Wonderful. She see anybody she *could* identify?"

"Two people."

"Who?"

"One was Dennis Pride. She didn't know his name, but she recognized him as Sherry's ex-husband."

"How did she know?"

"She's seen him around town. Restraining order or not, the guy practically lives here."

"Who else did she see?"

"The other guy was our private detective."

"Is she sure?"

"Recognized him from his picture in the paper."

"What did he do?"

"Hopped in his car, took off after the Japanese."

"The girl withheld this from me?"

"That's the wrong way to look at it, Chief."

"What's the *right* way to look at it?"

"The girl's *bringing* it to you. The girl's giving you all the facts. Some of the facts you were looking for. The detective followed them out of the Country Kitchen in his car."

"We *know* that," Harper said impatiently. "You said this girl had something. Tell me something I don't know."

Cora smiled. "She knows the *order.*"

Harper frowned. "Wait a minute. I thought she couldn't tell them apart."

"Hideki and Aoki, no. The woman left first with one, the other left alone. But *next* was Dennis Pride. The detective pulled out after him."

"Dennis got in *between* the detective and the people he was following?"

"That's right."

"That would tend to tick a detective off."

"It certainly would."

"A detective might pull a guy like that over, give him a piece of his mind."

"Not if it meant losing his quarry."

"Of course not," Harper agreed. "But say the lovebirds land. Dennis parks his car to spy on them. The detective walks up behind Dennis, says, 'What the hell are you doing?' Dennis picks up the samurai sword he's holding, and stabs the guy in the heart."

"After first carefully impaling it with a crossword puzzle and a sudoku? That makes no sense."

"No kidding. So someone comes along and sticks them on the sword after."

"The sudoku wasn't torn. The blade went right through. It wasn't slipped on the sword after. The sword had to go through the paper and into the body."

"Maybe, but the puzzle wasn't. You found it in the bushes."

"Even so."

"Even so what?"

"It doesn't matter if you slip one thing on the sword, or you slip two. The point is, with *anything* slipped on the sword, it's a whole new ball game."

"But it could have been done postmortem. Assuming Dennis is the killer. He could have killed him, and someone else could have come along and impaled the puzzles."

"Barney Nathan go along with that?"

"I haven't asked him."

"Whaddya wanna bet? The sword's out of the body now. You think he's going to swear it absolutely couldn't be done?"

"Are you trying to tell me Dennis did it?"

"Not at all. I'm just pointing out what a valuable witness this waitress will be to whoever gets charged with the crime. The defense attorney — who I'm assuming is Becky Baldwin in any case — will be able to call her to the stand and present her to the jury as reasonable doubt. Which is going to put the prosecutor in the rather embarrassing position of not being able to convict anyone. Probably even more embarrassing than arresting everyone and his brother and then turning them loose."

Chief Harper sighed. "You're telling me this witness is the kiss of death?"

"That's about the size of it."

"Gee. Thanks a lot."

CHAPTER 55

Dennis Pride looked sullen. Which wasn't surprising. He'd looked sullen ever since Sherry'd thrown him out. Even before Sherry'd thrown him out, actually. Dennis had a sullen nature, which projected okay with his rock band, but kind of sucked for everything else. He compensated with a winning smile, a handsome face, and the ability to charm the birds out of the trees. The fact he was still married, still employed, and not in jail were minor miracles, and a testament to the abilities of his attorney.

"I don't understand," Dennis griped.

"It's perfectly simple," Becky Baldwin said. "Cora Felton wants to ask you some questions. I'm here as your attorney looking out for your rights to make sure you don't get in trouble with your answers."

"Why does *she* get to ask me questions?"

"You mean since she has no legal standing?"

"Yeah."

"It's actually kind of nice. She has no legal right to ask you questions, and you have no obligation to answer. We're in my office instead of the police station. No one is taking anything down. You can't get into trouble, particularly since I won't let you. On the other hand, you may hear some things that might help. Cora?"

"All right, hotshot, here's the deal. I've uncovered a witness who saw you and the dead man leave the Country Kitchen at the same time on the night of the murder."

Dennis's eyes were wide. "What are you talking about?"

"I'm talking about the wonderful opportunity you had to kill the detective. So good, it's hard to believe you didn't do it. You still are claiming you didn't do it, aren't you?"

"What are you saying?"

"Great minds think alike. It seems you and the dead guy were following the same person. Does that ring a bell?"

"What is she talking about?" Dennis demanded from Becky.

"I'll give you a hint," Cora said. "He's Japanese."

"Are you just going to sit here and let her do this?"

Becky shrugged. "She's telling a story. She's not telling the police. She's just telling us. You can deny it, but for the moment, I'd like to hear it. Wouldn't you?"

"Sure you would," Cora said. "Tell you what. We'll talk hypothetically. A great big parenthetical hypothetical around the whole thing, so nothing you say can be used against you. Now, if you were following someone that night, who might that be?"

Dennis looked at Becky. "Why are you doing this again?"

Becky frowned. "It's a little complicated. Here's the deal. I'm doing this because she doesn't think you're guilty. The police don't either, but they have to act on the evidence. At the moment, it's important they don't get it. Our best shot — and understand this is not from the legal point of view — our best shot at clearing this up is telling Cora everything you know, so she can come up with a witness who helps you, instead of one who fries your ass. Like this one."

"Now then," Cora said. "You were pretty drunk when you left the Country Kitchen. You came to my house and told me you thought you were being followed. I don't buy that for a minute. That was just a ruse to get to see Sherry, wasn't it? Wasn't it?"

Dennis frowned. His face twisted. "I don't

know. I can't remember."

"You remember being in the Country Kitchen. Sitting in the bar."

"Yes."

"Why did you leave?"

Dennis looked at Becky.

"It's hypothetical, Dennis. Just tell her."

"Because he left."

"Who?"

"The Japanese guy. Son of a bitch."

"Why were you following him, Dennis?"

"The creep. Trying to pick up Sherry in the bar."

"Sherry wasn't there, Dennis."

"The other night. Sitting there. Getting her drunk. Good thing he let her go."

"So you were keeping tabs on him, to make sure he didn't hassle Sherry?"

"What's wrong with that?"

"Little ironic, don't you think?" Dennis glared. Cora said, "Never mind. You were in the bar with Hideki and Aoki and his wife. You followed them out to the parking lot. Reiko and the two men had a fight. They took off in their cars, and you followed."

"Yeah."

"What about the detective? Did you see him?"

"No."

"Are you sure?"

"No, I'm not sure. I'm not sure of any of this. You ask if I saw the detective. No, I didn't. At least, I don't remember seeing the detective. Hell, I didn't even know there *was* a detective."

"But you saw the others leave?"

"The guy and the girl. The one guy just stood there watching."

"I thought they all left together." Cora grimaced. "I don't mean *together.* In two cars. But at the same time."

Dennis shook his head. "No. He just stood there."

"Are you sure?"

"I almost ran him over."

"Okay. So when you pulled out of the lot. Was there another car between you and them?"

"I don't remember."

"How about behind you? Was there a car behind you?"

Dennis frowned, then nodded. "Yeah. Son of a bitch. Had his brights in my mirror." He pointed at Cora. "I *told* you I was being followed."

"He wasn't following you. He was following the car in front of you." Cora's eyes widened. "Oh, my God! That must have been Hideki! Hideki left with Reiko! You followed them, and the detective followed you."

Dennis shook his head. "No. I followed the man who had drinks with Sherry."

"He left with his wife?"

"He left with the woman."

"You're saying *Aoki* and Reiko were in the car you followed?"

"If that's their names."

"And the detective followed you?"

"*Someone* followed me."

"And it wasn't Hideki, because you nearly ran him over?"

"If that's his name."

Cora took a breath. "Dennis. You had a lot to drink. Both men were there that evening. You might have got confused."

"Now, at this point," Becky Baldwin said, "I think I might step in here. It's one thing for him to make a statement. It's another for you to cross-examine him on it."

"He's wrong."

"That's exactly what I can't have. He says one thing, you say another, and suddenly we're in that gray area where we don't want to be. I think Dennis has cooperated all he can. I'm certainly going to talk to him some more, but for the time being, you're through."

"Okay. I just want to be perfectly clear. As

far as Dennis is concerned, the Japanese man who left with the Japanese woman was the *same* Japanese man he saw having drinks with Sherry the night before."

Becky cocked her head. "Hypothetically?"

"Yes, hypothetically," Cora said irritably. "I think he's made that clear."

"I'm glad it's clear to you. Because I'm confused as hell." Cora got to her feet.

"Remember," Becky said. "This is totally off the record. You're not sharing any of this with Chief Harper."

Cora flashed her trademark Puzzle Lady smile. "Trust me."

CHAPTER 56

"I don't understand," Chief Harper said.

"Me either."

"If Dennis followed *Aoki* and his wife the whole thing makes no sense. I mean, it makes sense Dennis would follow *him,* since he was the guy drinking with Sherry. But why would the *detective* follow him? Detectives aren't hired to follow wives' husbands. They're hired to follow wives' lovers."

"No kidding. I remember when my husband, Henry, thought I had a thing for that jazz pianist —"

"Please! You think Dennis was right?"

"Good question. Dennis was drunk enough to mistake a closet for a men's room. On the other hand, when it's a guy after your girl, men have a surprising internal radar system. I would expect Dennis to get the right guy."

"So if Aoki left with his wife, where was Hideki?"

"*Not* leaving with Aoki's wife. Which must have been frustrating."

"And why was the detective following Aoki instead of Hideki?"

"Maybe wasn't hired to follow Hideki. Maybe he was hired to follow Mrs. Yoshiaki."

"So, who hired him?"

"Mr. Yoshiaki."

Harper frowned. "I don't like it. You think your wife is stepping out, you put a detective on her, sure. But when you know she's going to be with you most of the time, why do it? Particularly when you know the guy she's stepping out with. You put the tail on him. Then he's only around when it matters."

"I understand your theory. But say that's what happened. Aoki's coming here with his wife. Hideki's sniffing around. Aoki doesn't like it and puts a tail on him. Hideki notices the tail, freaks out, and kills him. Aoki's not pleased, but remembering the old adage, if at first you don't succeed, try, try again, he hires another private detective and puts him on the case. Hideki immediately kills him, after first carefully framing himself for the crime."

"That's ridiculous."

"No kidding. The only way it works is the

344

way we doped it out. Hideki kills the first detective. Aoki knows it, but Hideki's covered his tracks so well there's no way to prove it. What to do? Well, if the cops can't get him for a murder he did commit, he'll frame him for a murder he didn't. Aoki hires a second private detective, prepares a sudoku and crossword puzzle that names Hideki, takes his wife and hangs out in the Country Kitchen until Hideki shows up. He leaves with his wife. The detective follows. He takes her home to the bed-and-breakfast, drops her off. Goes out and confronts the detective. Says he has some instructions for him. Drives to the Tastee Freez, where he proceeds to do him in with a samurai sword."

"That Dennis stole from an antique shop," Chief Harper said ironically.

"Exactly," Cora said, ignoring the sarcasm. "Which he stole from the backseat of Dennis's car earlier that day by smashing the window."

"You say he dropped off his wife. No one at the bed-and-breakfast saw his wife coming home alone."

"Which means no one saw her, or she helped him do it."

"Helped him frame her lover?"

"Stranger things have happened."

"I'll say. In this case, stranger things happen every day."

"At any rate, he drives the guy to the Tastee Freez, and dispatches him with the samurai sword, carefully leaving the clues that will point to Hideki."

"The puzzle and the sudoku?"

"Right."

"And how does the puzzle get torn off the sword?"

Cora's eyes flicked. She recovered, said, "It tears off when he thrusts the sword in the body."

"And he doesn't notice?"

"Or Dennis pulls it off when he finds the body in a drunken stupor."

"Dennis?"

"Dennis had blood on his hands. We're assuming the murderer put it there to frame him. But what if he actually stumbled over the body?"

"Is there any evidence that he did?"

"Aside from the blood? Of course not. I'm just saying there's a lot of explanations for the torn puzzle. I wouldn't get too hung up on it."

"Oh, you wouldn't, would you?"

"No, I wouldn't. We know the puzzle goes with the sudoku because the one refers to the other. Without the puzzle, the sudoku is meaningless. In terms of the clue. The puzzle was there to begin with. How it got detached is beside the point."

"Uh-huh," Harper said. "And in this theory, Aoki kills the detective, leaves the puzzle and the sudoku to frame Hideki, but he puts blood on Dennis to frame him also?"

"You don't like that theory?"

"I hate that theory."

"Good. I hate it too. Aoki never did anything of the kind. He's my client, so he's innocent. Anything that indicates he isn't must be wrong."

"You believe that?"

"Hell, no. I'm not a lawyer. I'm an investigator. I'm working for my client. But if he's a killer, I'm not interested in covering it up."

"So you think he did it?"

"I have no idea who did it. We're laying out theories here. Based on this new information."

"What new information?"

"The gospel according to Dennis. We're taking his story at face value, and saying, if that's true, what happened?"

"And your theory is your client framed Hideki?"

"No, it's not. That's a terrible theory. Based on a horrible premise."

"What premise?"

"That two people committed the crimes. That one person killed the first detective, and another person killed the second. When that happens in a mystery, the writer is usually taken out and shot. On the other hand, the theory Aoki committed both crimes is worse. He hires one detective, doesn't like the job he's done, so he kills him. He'd like to frame it on Hideki, but he's not prepared. So he *gets* prepared. Hires another detective, and carries out the frame." Cora made a face. "Pee-ew! No way that works."

"Yes, but we don't know the facts."

"No kidding. What works best is if Aoki hires the first detective and Hideki kills him. What doesn't work is Aoki hiring the second detective. Unless he's hiring him to frame Hideki, like we said, which gets into the whole two separate murderers bit."

"What if Hideki hired the detectives?"

"Why?"

"To keep tabs on Aoki's wife. Tip him off when she was alone."

Cora considered. "I like it."

"You think it's right?"

"No, I think it's wrong. But I admire the deviousness of your mind. The *husband* doesn't hire the detective to keep tabs on his wife. The *lover* hires him. A wonderful variation. Just the right nuance."

"Then why don't you like it?"

"Give me a break. The husband notices he's being followed and kills the guy?"

"No," Harper said. "The husband notices his *wife's* being followed and kills the guy."

"Why?"

"What do you mean, why? He doesn't want anyone following his wife."

"Why not?"

"Are you being irritating deliberately?"

"It's the facts that are irritating you, Chief. You say this guy killed the detective for following his wife. That doesn't cut it for me. I can't imagine him doing it. And if he did, I can't imagine she wouldn't know about it. This is a husband and wife we're talking about. Surely this is the sort of thing that would come up in dinner conversation. 'By the way, I killed the detective your lover had following you. Pass the salt.' "

"I just said what if Hideki hired the PI. I didn't say what if Aoki killed him."

"You think Hideki hired him *and* killed him?" Cora shrugged. "I suppose that's one way to get free service. Keep hiring PIs and bumpin' 'em off before they get paid. You'd think after a few of those, the PI'd want his money in advance."

"No fair. You're sitting here ridiculing

every idea."

"Because none of them work, Chief. You got a bunch of bad ideas kicking around. It's not like you can pick one and say, 'That works.' Nothing works. Every idea you throw out is going to be bad."

"How about *you* throw out some ideas and let *me* ridicule them?"

"I thought I did. And they all stink. The idea Hideki hired the detectives is ridiculous. The idea he hired one and Aoki hired the other is even more ridiculous. The idea Aoki hired both of them is better, but not much. I could see him hiring the first one. I can't see him hiring the second. Unless he hired him to kill him to set up Hideki." Cora considered. "What about his wife?"

"Huh?"

"You're leaving her out of this. But what if she's the driving force?"

"She hires the detective to follow herself?"

"To follow her *husband.* To let her know what *he's* up to. To keep him away from her and Hideki."

"She hired both detectives and her husband killed both detectives just to put her in her place?"

"You enjoy ridiculing, don't you, Chief?"

Harper grinned. He was in a much better

mood by the time Dan Finley called, pleased as punch, to say he'd found the car.

CHAPTER 57

The PI's car was in the deep underbrush behind the old paper mill, a half mile north of the Tastee Freez. The overgrown service road was almost never used, except as a lovers' lane. Searching the woods around it had been an inspired guess.

"You sure it's his car?" Harper said.

Dan seemed offended by the question. "It's his license plate," he said, somewhat defensively.

"You search the car?"

"It's locked."

"You didn't jimmy the door?"

"I waited for you."

"Good man. Do me a favor. Don't tell the TV guys till we check it out."

Harper, Dan, and Cora picked their way through the underbrush. Cora's legs were getting all scratched up by nettles, but she wasn't about to miss it. She was right behind when the officers reached the car.

Chief Harper pulled on thin rubber gloves. "Don't touch anything," he warned. He took out a metal jimmy, fitted it in the crack in the driver's-side window, popped the door.

The horrendous wail of a car alarm filled the air.

Harper reached in, fiddled with something under the dashboard, and the wailing stopped.

"That's pretty neat," Cora said. "I don't suppose you could show me how to do that?"

Harper gave her a look. He leaned down, popped the latch. Walked around to the back and raised the trunk.

Dan whistled.

Cora leaned forward to look.

It was an old ax. The wooden handle was rotten and covered with moss. Like something pulled off a junk heap.

The blade was crusted with dried blood.

Harper nodded. "That's our weapon, all right. Looks like the killer just used it because it was there." He frowned. "I don't mean that as dumb as it sounds."

"It won't sound dumb to a defense attorney. It would argue against premeditation. Anything else?"

"No. Let's check out the seats."

The front seat yielded nothing but some rather foul air. Harper popped the rear door. Cora peered in. There was nothing on the seat, but there was something in the shadows on the floor.

Chief Harper leaned over her shoulder. "What's that?"

"I don't know. But it smells like hell."

"Hang on," Dan said, "I got a flashlight."

Dan pulled the light off his belt, shone it on the floor.

It was a human eye.

Chapter 58

"What does the car tell us?"

"I'm glad you asked me that."

"Why?"

"It means I can smoke." Cora reached in her purse, took out her cigarettes.

Harper didn't even put up a token resistance. He tipped back in his desk chair, said, "Come on. What does it mean?"

Cora lit a cigarette, blew out the match. "The car tells us a lot. It's not that far from the Tastee Freez. Whoever ditched it probably walked back to the Tastee Freez. Which means the killing took place at the Tastee Freez."

"In that case," Harper said, "why isn't the body in the car? You're gonna ditch the car, why don't you ditch the body?"

"It could be a lot of reasons. One, the killer wants it found."

"Why?"

"Say it was incriminating. Not to the

killer. To someone the killer wanted to incriminate."

"Who?"

"Exactly. Body in the boondocks is a sticky problem for *X*. *X* equals guilty-looking-innocent-person. Solve for *X*."

"That's no help at all."

"No. But it's nice to have the problem correctly stated."

"What's another reason?"

"Expedience. The guy wasn't killed in the car. So when the killer ditches the car, the body's not in it."

"But the guy's eye *is?*"

"Of course it is. If the eye's found with the body, it's obvious the murder took place there. The killer wants to make it look like the body was dumped. The eye's gotta go, so the killer throws it in the car. Same with the murder weapon. So we won't know where the guy was killed."

"But when we find it in the car, we'll know. So why not just get rid of it?"

"We'll know anyway. If the body was dumped, the guy's car is most likely gathering parking tickets somewhere in Manhattan. The minute we find the car close to the crime scene, it's clear what happened, eye or no eye. So why bother ditching it elsewhere? Which couldn't be much fun. Of course, I'm no expert. I've never disposed of an eye."

"What's the point of ditching the car at all? The killer must know it's going to be found."

"Yeah, but not for a while. Ditching the car serves two purposes. It will be longer before the body's found, and longer before the car's found. The killer doesn't mind if they're found, he just doesn't want them found right away."

"Why?"

"Gee, I don't know. Can you think of anyone who's visiting town, and won't be here long?"

"So, we're back to the Japanese."

Cora shrugged. "Who else had reason to hire a detective?"

"I have no idea." Harper sighed. "This is the point where you whip out the crossword puzzle, solve it, and tell me who to arrest."

"Been there, done that. The crossword puzzle fingers Hideki. You've arrested him already."

"I know." Harper cocked his head. "What about the other puzzle?"

"What other puzzle?"

"The one we found in the safe."

Cora made a face. "That was a stupid

Puzzle Lady puzzle. It didn't mean anything."

"Stupid?"

"Hey, just because it pays the rent doesn't
mean I gotta like it."

"The puzzle was in the guy's safe. It ought
to mean something."

"I solved it. It doesn't."

Harper got up, went to the file cabinet.

"What are you doing?"

"It's not that I don't trust your hunches,"
Harper said, "but this is personal. It's your
column. It's your puzzle. You're apt to be
influenced."

"It's a puzzle in the paper. If it means
anything, I'll eat it."

Harper took out a plastic evidence bag
with the newspaper inside. "Okay, can you
solve it again?"

A chill ran down Cora's spine. Did she
remember what the puzzle said enough to
fill it in? Not likely.

She kept her cool. "All that matters is the
theme answer," she said, smoothly. "That's,
'If he cries, and feels low. He needs help.
Help him go.' It's advice on how to deal
with a moody, annoying ex, and doesn't
mean a damn thing."

"Suppose it wasn't the crossword puzzle,"
Chief Harper said, "which made the paper

important. Suppose it was something else. Like the headline on page one."

Cora picked up the plastic envelope, said, "May I?"

"Be my guest."

Cora slid the newspaper out, flipped it open to the front page. "Well, for one thing, this is the *Bakerhaven Gazette*."

"Really?"

"You didn't notice? Well, it is. That's a pretty good indication whoever hired the detective either lives in Bakerhaven or was in Bakerhaven when the paper came out."

"Which is what we figured," Harper said. "Anything else?"

"Not much. Coverage of the war. National news. Nothing even remotely connected to anything here or in New York. And —"

"What?"

"This is *Wednesday's* paper."

"So?"

"The detective was *dead* Wednesday." Cora held up the newspaper. "How did this get in his safe?"

Chapter 59

Aaron was defensive. "Why do you want to know?"

"Are you kidding? This is a murder case."

"I don't see what this has to do with it."

Cora Felton jerked her thumb toward the door of Aaron's office. "Want me to ask your editor?"

"Leave my editor alone. It's bad enough you barging in here when I should be working. How am I going to get married if you get me fired?"

"How are you going to get married if you keep brushing off the bride?"

"Excuse me?"

"You think you're acting in Sherry's best interests. You're not. You're reacting to Dennis, and it's stupid as hell. Dennis doesn't *want* Sherry to get married. He wants to throw a monkey wrench into the plans. And you're helping him do it. Every time you run around acting like a jealous nitwit, Dennis wins. You've been acting pretty stupid lately."

"Now, look here."

Cora put up her hands. "No. We're beyond that. Way beyond that. We've got two murders, more suspects than you can shake a stick at, and a whole bunch of clues that don't add up. I'm trying to sort things out, and, believe me, it isn't easy. So quit stalling and give me a straight answer."

Aaron frowned. "When do we go to press?"

"That's the *question*. What's the *answer*?"

"It depends. A normal day, we're rolling by five or six. If something's breaking, it might not be till midnight."

"Once you're rolling, how soon before the first paper comes off the press? Say you wanted to bring a copy home."

"I wouldn't do that."

"Why not?"

"I get it delivered," Aaron said. "Why should I wait around?"

"Why indeed? But it wouldn't be that long, would it?"

"Not at all. Why?"

Cora ignored the question. "Look, Aaron. I need your cooperation. Here's the deal. I've got to solve this thing, and to do that I need Dennis here."

Aaron opened his mouth to protest, but Cora cut him off. "I don't want to hear it. I know what I have to do. I'm going to take legal action. It won't be easy, and I can't have you messing things up. So how about it? Can I count on you? Because I really need your help."

Aaron exhaled. "All right. What do you want me to do?"

Cora shrugged. "Why don't you confess?"

CHAPTER 60

Judge Hobbs looked out over the crowded courtroom and frowned. Every available seat was filled, people were standing in the back, and Rick Reed and the channel 8 news team were covering the proceedings.

"Why are we here?" the elderly jurist demanded.

Cora Felton, clad in her finest Miss Marple attire, curtsied and smiled. "Your Honor. I am here to petition the court for a stay in the matter of the restraining order prohibiting Dennis Pride from coming within a hundred yards of his ex-wife, Sherry Carter."

"You want me to lift the restraining order?"

"Temporarily, Your Honor. Just temporarily, until we can clear things up. You will take note Mr. Pride is seated at the defense table with his attorney, Ms. Baldwin, and his present wife, Brenda Wallenstein Pride."

"If he's seeking to lift the restraining order, why isn't Ms. Baldwin speaking for him?"

Becky rose. "He's not seeking to lift the restraining order, Your Honor."

"No?"

"No."

"Then who is?"

"I am, Your Honor," Cora said, "on behalf of my niece, Sherry Carter."

"Your niece is seeking to lift the restraining order?"

"Yes."

"Then why isn't she here?"

Cora smiled. "Because of the restraining order, Your Honor. My niece is not allowed within a hundred yards of her ex-husband. Your courtroom is not large enough for the two of them to occupy it at one time. If he's in here, she has to wait outside."

"Oh, for goodness sakes," Judge Hobbs said, irritably. "And who are all these people who *are* here?"

"Witnesses, Your Honor."

"Witnesses to what?"

"Various aspects of the case."

"What case?"

"The case I propose to present."

"You're not presenting a case."

"Yes, I am, Your Honor. I'm presenting

evidence why the restraining order should be temporarily lifted."

"For how long?"

"Oh. I hadn't thought of that. Not long, Your Honor. Say twenty-four hours."

"Then you don't *need* witnesses. I will suspend the restraining order for twenty-four hours on my own accord."

District Attorney Henry Firth rose from the prosecution table, his ratty nose twitching. "I oppose that, Your Honor."

Judge Hobbs's mouth fell open. "You what?"

"As the prosecutor, I must strongly oppose such arbitrary action. I insist the restraining order be kept in place."

"Why would you do that?"

"I have heard no reason why it shouldn't. This is a serious matter, Your Honor. I must point out that the subject in question is on probation, that the restraining order is one of the provisions of that probation, that breaking the restraining order is grounds for sending the subject in question to jail to serve out his sentence for conviction of —"

Becky Baldwin sprang to her feet. "Object to my client's record being paraded through open court."

"How can you object to that when you're asking that his restraining order be lifted?"

Judge Hobbs protested.

"I'm *not* asking his restraining order be lifted, Your Honor." Becky order pointed at Cora. "*She* is."

Judge Hobbs threw up his hands. "God save me!"

"It's simple, Your Honor," Henry Firth said. "The prosecution is not about to lift a restraining order on Miss Felton's say-so. If she has evidence, let her produce it."

"I do, Your Honor."

"Harumph," Judge Hobbs said. "This is most irregular."

"If I might make a suggestion," Cora ventured.

"Yes, Ms. Felton."

"If Your Honor could temporarily waive the restraining order, pending your decision whether or not you will temporarily waive the restraining order, my niece could come into court."

"You want me to temporarily suspend the ruling we are discussing temporarily suspending?"

"It affects my niece, Your Honor. She ought to be here."

"Bring her in," Judge Hobbs said. "I will take judicial cognizance of the fact she is entering my courtroom. I do not wish to have her proximity to her ex-husband pointed out to me. Anyone whipping out a tape measure will be ejected from the court. Is that acceptable, Ms. Baldwin?"

"Yes, Your Honor."

"Any objection from the prosecution?"

"No objection to Ms. Carter being allowed into the courtroom. However, I strongly object to waiving the restraining order."

"Any objection to waiving the restraining order while we debate it?" Judge Hobbs asked drily.

"If I say no, will Your Honor not take that as a concession that I am yielding the point?"

"Never mind," Judge Hobbs said. "Don't say yes. Don't say no. Stand mute. I assure you, your doing so will not reflect one way or another on any matter that might be decided today. Chief Harper, bring the young lady in. If anyone tries to stop you, arrest them."

Sherry Carter, accompanied by Aaron Grant, was ushered in. Harper moved the camera crew to make room for them.

"All right," Judge Hobbs said. "Now that we've finally admitted the only person in Bakerhaven *not* to be present in my courtroom, let's deal with those people who are. Ms. Felton, are you prepared to proceed?"

"Yes, Your Honor. At this time I would like to petition the court to lift the restraining order on Dennis Pride."

"Opposed, Your Honor," Henry Firth said.

"Very well. Ms. Felton, do you have any evidence to support your petition?"

Cora smiled. "Do I ever."

CHAPTER 61

Cora strode out into the middle of the court. "For my first witness I would like to call Dennis Pride."

Judge Hobbs smiled. "Ah. That's a refreshing change. Calling the very person your petition concerns. Perhaps we can clear up this matter."

"I certainly hope so, Your Honor."

Dennis took the witness stand.

"Mr. Pride, you were arrested for the murder of Lester Mathews."

"Objection," Becky said. "Anyone can be arrested."

"Sustained. Ms. Felton, you can't impeach a witness by showing he's been arrested. Only convictions are relevant."

"I'm not trying to impeach him, Your Honor. That was merely preliminary."

"I don't care what phase of the testimony it was. Keep it within the law."

"Mr. Pride, do you have an agreement

with the prosecutor regarding immunity?"

"Objection."

"Overruled. Witness may answer."

"I am a prosecution witness. The prosecutor has granted me immunity to anything that might technically or otherwise violate my probation."

"That was for acts already done, wasn't it?"

Dennis frowned. "I beg your pardon?"

"He granted you immunity from prosecution for anything you might have *done.* In the *past.* This wasn't a blank check to go out and do anything you felt like because you had immunity."

"No. Of course not."

"That was two days ago. So anything you've done in the past two days the cops could nail you on. Isn't that right, Mr. Prosecutor?"

"Objection," Henry Firth said. "*I'm* not the witness. I'm not the one being questioned here."

"You should be," Cora said. "You're the one who granted immunity."

Judge Hobbs banged the gavel. "That will do. We will have no more asides. The point is valid. Unless anyone wishes to argue it. Even if they do, the point is valid. The witness was granted immunity. That immunity ends as of the time it was granted. No acts committed *after* the grant of immunity are *covered* by the grant of immunity. Is that clear?"

"Would that include violating the restraining order?" Becky said. "Because, if so, I am going to suggest that my client leave the stand and not say another word until I have had a chance to talk to the prosecutor."

"That would seem the prudent course of action," Judge Hobbs observed.

"There's no need," Henry Firth said. "I'm willing to stipulate that my immunity with regard to the restraining order shall extend until such time as the court shall rule on whether or not to lift it."

"With that assurance, may we proceed?"

"Absolutely," Becky said.

"Great," Cora said. "On the night of the murder of the second private eye, Lester Mathews, you were in the bar of the Country Kitchen, were you not?"

"Yes, I was."

"You were there when Mr. Yoshiaki left with his wife?"

"That's right."

"You're sure it was Mr. Yoshiaki?"

"Yes, I am."

"How can you be sure?"

"Because I saw him the night before. Talking to my ex-wife."

"Where was this?"

"Same place. The Country Kitchen bar."

"You're sure it was the same man?"

"Yes, I am."

"It couldn't have been another Asian man you mistook for him?"

"All Asians don't look alike."

"I didn't say they do. I'm asking if it's possible you made a mistake?"

"No. I saw him leaving with his wife."

"What did you do?"

"I followed him."

"Why?"

"To see if he went home with his wife. Or if he dropped her off and went out again."

"What did he do?"

"I don't know."

"Why not?"

"I lost him."

"But you followed him when he left the Country Kitchen?"

"That's right."

"Did you see anyone *else* following him when he left the Country Kitchen?"

"No, I did not."

"The detective who was killed. You didn't see the detective follow him?"

"No, I did not."

"Your witness," Cora said.

Henry Firth stood up, smiled. "No questions," he said, and sat down.

Judge Hobbs frowned. "No questions?"

"None, Your Honor."

"I don't understand. You oppose the motion, yet you have no questions?"

"I haven't heard anything I need to challenge. Has Your Honor heard anything that would warrant lifting the restraining order?"

"I'm not the one being questioned," Judge Hobbs said testily.

"I beg your pardon, Your Honor."

"Do you have any more witnesses?"

"I have several, Your Honor," Cora said.

"I'd like to expedite this. Who do you intend to call?"

"Let's see. I have Aoki, and Aoki's wife, Reiko. I have Hideki Takiyama. I have Mary Dobbs, a waitress from the Country Kitchen, Mr. Meachem, the owner of Meachem's Antique Shop, Mrs. Clemson who lives across the street from him, Mr. and Mrs. Jacobson, from Jacobson's bed-and-breakfast, Mr. and Mrs. Murdock from Murdock's bed-and-breakfast. I have Harvey Beerbaum, who will interpret some puzzles, Barney Nathan, medical examiner, who can testify to the time of death."

"Wait a minute. What time of death? We're talking about a restraining order. All of these people are irrelevant."

"Not at all, Your Honor. The restraining order on Dennis Pride is interfering with the solution to two murders. It needs to be lifted."

"Which I vigorously oppose," the prosecutor said.

Judge Hobbs frowned. "On what grounds? Don't you want these murders solved?"

"I dispute the premise. The one thing has nothing to do with the other. I can solve these crimes without Dennis Pride's help."

"Really?" Cora said. "At the moment you have Mr. Yoshiaki charged with them. Do you actually think he did it?"

"The evidence would so indicate."

"You're basing that on Mr. Pride's testimony?"

"What if I am?"

"Then you better lift Mr. Pride's restraining order."

Judge Hobbs's gavel came down with force. "That will do! What are you, children? I would think you both know better."

"Sorry, Your Honor," Cora said. "I was putting on witnesses. May I proceed?"

"You're going to call all these people?"

"I hope not, Your Honor. I'm going to call as many as necessary. Call Aoki Yoshiaki."

Aoki got up, was sworn, took the stand.

Judge Hobbs frowned at him suspiciously, addressed the prosecutor. "Mr. Firth. Correct me if I'm wrong, but is this not the gentleman you have currently charged with the crimes?"

"Yes, Your Honor."

"The prosecution has no objection to his testifying at this time?"

"Absolutely not, Your Honor. We welcome it."

"Well, his *attorney* should object. Ms. Baldwin. You are Mr. Yoshiaki's attorney of record?"

"That's right, Your Honor."

"Yet you're also appearing for Mr. Pride."

"Yes, I am."

"Isn't that a conflict of interest?"

"No, Your Honor."

"Are you willing to allow Mr. Yoshiaki to testify?"

"Yes, Your Honor."

"While he's a defendant in a murder case?"

"That's right, Your Honor."

"There you are. We have an obvious conflict of interest, and that proves it."

"No, it doesn't Your Honor," Cora said.

Judge Hobbs nearly struck himself with his gavel. "I beg your pardon?"

"It's not a conflict of interest. Ms. Baldwin

is perfectly capable of looking out for Mr. Yoshiaki's interests. I'm sure she will object to any question that might incriminate him. I appreciate your concern, but I assure you there is no problem."

"Very well," Judge Hobbs said. "But be careful."

"Thank you, Your Honor. Mr. Yoshiaki, are you acquainted with Dennis Pride, the subject of this petition?"

"No, I am not."

"Have you seen him before?"

"Yes."

"Where would that be?"

"In the bar of the Country Kitchen."

"On what occasion?"

"The night he saw me there."

"With Sherry Carter?"

"No. With my wife. The night I was there with my wife."

"The night he claims he followed you?"

"Yes."

"Did you see him following you?"

"No."

"*Would* you have seen someone following you?"

He frowned. "I do not understand the question."

"Were you paying attention to see if anyone was following you? Did you think that was a possibility?"

"No."

"When you got in the car with your wife, where did you go?"

"To the bed-and-breakfast. Where we are staying."

"Murdock's bed-and-breakfast?"

"If that is their name."

"The people sitting right there. Are they the owners of the bed-and-breakfast? The people who rented you the room?"

"Yes, they are."

"Did you see them that night when you went into the bed-and-breakfast with your wife?"

"Objection," Becky said. "That's leading and suggestive and assumes facts not in evidence. No one has testified that he went inside with his wife, or that he encountered the Murdocks when he did."

"That's why they're here to testify," Cora said. "But I don't want to clutter up the stand with an unnecessary parade of witnesses. I'll withdraw the question, and ask another. Mr. Yoshiaki, you're acquainted with Hideki Takiyama?"

"Yes."

"Are you aware he was born in America?" As the witness hesitated, Cora added, "I remind you, I heard you make a remark to that effect."

"I am aware of it, yes."

"As an American citizen, he has a Social Security number. Do you know it?"

"The Social Security number?"

"Yes."

"No. Why should I?"

"It has been suggested you used it to frame him."

"I did not. That is ridiculous."

"That's how it seems to you?"

"Yes, it is."

"Okay. Then let's ask him."

Cora dismissed Aoki and called Hideki to the stand.

"Mr. Takiyama, why did you come here to this town?"

"I came to sign you to a contract to write a sudoku book."

"Did you do so?"

"No, I did not."

"Why is that?"

"Mr. Yoshiaki learned of my plans, and got there first."

"Did this make you mad?"

"It was not honorable."

"You believe in honor?"

"Yes, I do."

"Do you know Aoki's wife?"

"I know Reiko."

"What do you think of her?"

"She is a fine woman. It is a shame that she made a bad marriage."

"And Dennis Pride, the subject of this petition? Are you acquainted with him?"

"I do not know him. I know who he is."

"Did you ever try to kill him?"

There were gasps in the courtroom, followed by a low rumble that swelled into a din.

Judge Hobbs banged the gavel.

Hideki, shocked by the question, had time to recover. "Of course not."

"With the samurai sword you stole from his car. Did you ever try to kill him with that?"

"Samurai sword *I* stole. . . . ?"

"From his car. Yes. *That* samurai sword. Isn't that why you stole it?"

"I did not steal the samurai sword!"

"And if a witness saw you take it from his car . . . ?"

"They are lying! *You* are lying! There is no witness! I did not take it!"

"Really?" Cora frowned. "That's funny. I thought you stole the sword to kill Dennis Pride."

"Nonsense. I do not know the man. Why would I kill him?"

"To frame Aoki for his murder." Cora

379

smiled. "You stole the sword from Dennis Pride. You got Aoki's fingerprints on it by leaning it up against the door of his car. He had to move it to get in. Which was all you needed. You retrieved the sword, stashed it in the trunk of your car. When Dennis followed Aoki and Reiko, you tagged along behind. All you had to do was wait until Dennis followed them home, then kill him with the sword. The inference would be obvious. Aoki caught Dennis following him, and killed him.

"Why didn't that happen? Because Dennis was so drunk, he pulled off the side of the road and went to sleep. Thereby saving his life.

"So you killed the detective instead."

Hideki smiled sarcastically. "What detective? That is what I would like to know. Yes, I know there is a detective, and I know that he is dead. What I do not know is why he was killed."

"He was killed to frame you. So the sudoku and the crossword puzzle could be left on the body to frame you for the crime." Cora spread her arms, smiled at the judge, and the courtroom, and the TV camera. "Which was really the *frame of the frame*. You framed yourself, to make it look like Aoki was framing you."

380

"That is ridiculous!"

"Actually, it's rather clever. You can console yourself with that while you're in jail."

Judge Hobbs leaned forward on the bench. "Miss Felton, can you prove this?"

"Absolutely, Your Honor." Cora turned back to Hideki. "I have an eyewitness."

"Impossible! I did not do it!"

"You did, and I can prove it. I know exactly what happened. It was easy. All you had to do was surprise the detective on stakeout, stab him with the samurai sword, run the body out to the Tastee Freez, and set up a scene that would resemble the first murder. You'd leave a crossword puzzle and a sudoku that implicated you, and it would look like Aoki was trying to frame you for the crime.

"What you didn't plan on was Dennis Pride waking up."

Consternation showed on Hideki's face.

"See, Dennis was the joker in the deck. When Aoki left the Country Kitchen, Dennis tagged along. So did the detective. Dennis was pretty drunk. He passed out in his car. He thought he had a nightmare, the vision he had of an Asian man killing a Caucasian. It's only lately he's come to realize this was not a drunken hallucination, but something he'd actually seen." Cora smiled. "You see why it's so important the restraining order be lifted? Dennis Pride will be the chief witness against you. To the fact that you killed the detective and framed yourself with cryptic puzzles to make it look like your rival was framing you. It might have worked, except for one thing. The eyewitness. Dennis saw you do it."

"That is a lie!" Hideki snarled. His lip curled back, stretching his scar. "He was dead drunk! He did not see a thing!"

A hush fell over the courtroom.

Cora smiled. "No, but you did. Didn't you, Hideki? *You're* the eyewitness. You saw Dennis passed out in his car. You just said so. *He was dead drunk and didn't see a thing.* And you're absolutely right. Dennis didn't see *you* at the scene of the crime. You saw *him. You're* the eyewitness who places you there."

Hideki blinked, as the realization hit him. He sat in stunned silence, overwhelmed, unable to think of a single thing to say.

Cora spread her arms, and curtsied to the judge.

"I rest my case."

CHAPTER 62

Chief Harper frowned at the gathering in his office. "What are Sherry and Aaron doing here? Not that I don't like you kids, but we have business."

"So do we, Chief," Cora said. "And I'd like to get it taken care of before anything else pops up. Aaron has a confession to make. You and Sherry need to hear it. I'm not sure anyone else does. It looks like you got Hideki dead to rights. But if he hires a good defense attorney . . ."

"Becky's not representing him?"

"Just until another attorney can be found. She's recusing herself on the grounds that she helped trap him."

"Becky was in on it?"

"Did I say that, Chief? Becky's actions, however innocent, may have inadvertently led to his arrest. There's a fine line here, Chief. She wasn't his attorney at the time. She had been his attorney. Then she got him out of jail. When he no longer needed her services, she contracted them to Aoki. In the course of defending Mr. Yoshiaki, it came to pass that —"

Harper put up his hands. "Save it for the judge. I just asked if she was defending him. If he gets outside counsel, it's all well and good. Now, what is it you're hoping won't have to come out?"

"I hired the detective," Aaron said.

Harper's eyes narrowed. "Are you kidding me?"

"No, he did it, the big lug," Sherry said. "Isn't that the stupidest thing you ever heard?"

"You can fight it out later, kids," Cora said. "Right now, let's move things along. Aaron hired the detective to keep an eye on Dennis. Dennis was hanging around, getting drunk, spying on Sherry, and smashing his headlight."

"Headlight?"

"Aaron thinks Dennis broke his headlight. He was going to report it, but Sherry and I talked him out of it. Actually, we got distracted by Hideki and Aoki performing the Japanese version of *High Noon*."

"You mentioned moving things along," Harper pointed out.

"Right. Aaron couldn't keep tabs on

Dennis because he has a job. The dead PI gave him the idea. He could hire a guy to watch him."

"Indefinitely?" Chief Harper said skeptically.

"Exactly," Sherry said. "See how stupid?"

"Not indefinitely," Aaron said. "Until he violated probation and went to jail."

"Stick with me here," Cora said. "Never mind if it was a smart move, the fact is he did it. Tuesday afternoon, Aaron spotted Dennis's car in front of the Country Kitchen. He wasn't about to confront him. He'd taken enough lumps for that. He went back to the paper, called a PI. Lester Mathews. Asked him to follow the guy.

"Well, Mathews doesn't know Aaron Grant from Adam — Aaron picked the PI's name out of a phone book — and the guy's not going to drive all the way to Bakerhaven on Aaron's say-so. He wants cash. Aaron won't give him a credit card number — Aaron doesn't want any record of the transaction — so he has to hire him in person. He rushes to the PI's office, gives him two hundred dollars. And, because Aaron doesn't want to leave his card, what does he leave instead?"

"The *Bakerhaven Gazette*?"

"Hot off the press. With the paper's phone

number, and his byline. Wednesday's paper, which he got Tuesday night. Accounting for how it got in the dead man's safe."

"Why is it open to the crossword puzzle?"

"My picture. Aaron's got photos of Sherry, but he doesn't carry one of me. He wants the guy to know who we are, in case Dennis bumps into us."

"You're talking about me as if I weren't here," Aaron said.

"Believe me, it's for your own good. Anyway, Aaron leads the PI back to the Country Kitchen and points out Dennis to him. Not realizing he was sending the guy to his death."

"Hey. I feel bad enough already."

"I'm sure you do. I just want to rub it in, in case this is the only time you get blamed for it. How about it, Chief? Can we leave this alleged hiring alone until someone raises the issue?"

"Why cover it up?"

"Oh. Bad choice of language. We're not covering anything up. We're simply not volunteering extraneous information that has nothing to do with the price of beans. Why? Because the ex-husband from hell will file it away under *P for persecuted,* and it will be tough to argue with, since it actually happened."

Harper frowned.

"Believe me, you do not want to give that son of a bitch cause to play the martyr." Cora smiled. "On the bright side, I never did get that restraining order lifted, so you got every right in the world to kick him out of town."

Harper said, "Do you realize what you're asking?"

"I'm not asking anything. I'm in here giving you a hypothetical situation. In the event that Aaron Grant had done so-and-so, would it be possible for you to do such-and-such?"

"I don't recall you saying this was hypothetical."

"I'm sure I did. Anyway, being a nice guy and all, if you do choose such-and-such, you'd surely give Aaron a heads-up so he knows how to handle himself and what to put in the paper." Cora waved her hands. "Come on, kids. No more stalling. Go see the Reverend Kimble and set a date."

After Sherry and Aaron left, Chief Harper said, "He really did that?"

"Damn right. And I'm glad of it. It was the missing piece in the puzzle. Remember the problem I had? If Aoki hired the first detective, I couldn't see him hiring the second? On the other hand, I couldn't see

Hideki hiring the detective just to set up the pseudo-frame? Well, throw Aaron Grant into the equation, and the whole thing is simple. Aoki hired a detective to keep an eye on Hideki. Hideki doesn't take kindly to being followed, and caves the detective's head in. An impulsive act, of the type Hideki's been committing. This time he goes too far. Winds up with a one-eyed gumshoe and a bloody mess.

"Oops.

"What is he to do? If the cops start snooping around, find out the detective was hired to follow him, he's not just the number-one suspect, he's bought a first-class ticket up the river.

"He'd love to ditch the body, but he's not too keen on driving around with a corpse in the car. But the body's not *in* the car. So what if he doesn't ditch the body, what if he just ditches the car? If he gets rid of the car it will look like the body was brought here and dumped.

"So he throws the ax in the trunk of the car, and the bloody eye on the floor of the backseat."

"Why?" Harper asked.

"He doesn't want to leave the murder weapon with the body, or it will look like a crime scene, instead of a place it was dumped. Same thing with the eye. It's lying next to the corpse, screaming, 'Look, look, someone whacked me on the head right here!' He throws it in the car, and hides the car in the woods. Far enough so it won't be found for a while, but close enough for him to walk back.

"Anyway, ditching the car is such a good strategy the case makes barely a ripple in Bakerhaven. Aoki doesn't even hear about it. When he takes Sherry out and signs her to a contract, he thinks the PI's still working for him.

"By the time Aoki finds out the PI's been murdered, he's sure Hideki did it, but there's nothing he can do. He can't accuse Hideki without admitting he hired the PI. Which he absolutely will not. It wouldn't be honorable. It would be admitting he didn't trust his wife. Even after he's arrested for murder, Aoki won't admit to hiring the PI, even to his lawyer.

"Anyway, after he kills the PI, Hideki is upset. Not in the normal way, because Hideki's not a normal person. He's upset that Aoki won't get blamed for it. Aoki hired the detective. There ought to be some way to connect him to the crime. If he'd only been prepared to do it.

"Hideki's no slow learner. Next time he

will be prepared. Aaron's account of the crime mentions the victim had a crossword puzzle and a sudoku in his pocket. They don't mean anything, they're just puzzles in the paper, but they give Hideki the idea. So he creates a sudoku and a crossword puzzle that, taken together, yield his Social Security number. He goads Aoki in the street to make a crack about his birthright, establishing Aoki knows he's a U.S. citizen, and laying the groundwork for setting Aoki up for the frame. He steals a samurai sword, leans it against the door of Aoki's car, to get his fingerprints on it. He retrieves the sword, waits for his chance.

"It doesn't take long. That night, he, Aoki, and Reiko have a huge dustup in the bar, witnessed by everyone, during which Dennis staggers up to Aoki and accuses him of making a play for Sherry.

"Which couldn't be better. When Dennis follows them out to the parking lot, the stage is set. Dennis will follow Aoki. Hideki will kill Dennis with the samurai sword with Aoki's fingerprints on it. Dennis is the guy who had the sword in the first place. The inference will be clear. Dennis stole the sword, and Aoki took it away from him and killed him with it.

"Why doesn't he?

"The outside event.

"The private detective Aaron hired to keep tabs on Dennis.

"There's no way Hideki knows that. When Dennis takes off after Aoki, and the detective takes off after him, Hideki is baffled. He thinks the detective is following Aoki. Why, he has no idea. Most likely he figures the guy was hired to follow *him* and couldn't tell one Asian from another.

"What happens? Dennis pulls off the road, passes out. The private eye pulls off the road too. Hideki can't kill Dennis with a witness. No matter. He kills the private eye."

"In front of Dennis?" Harper said.

"Why not? Dennis was passed out. If he saw anything, he'd think it was a traumatic, repressed nightmare. Hideki sneaks up behind the private eye, stabs him in the heart.

"Now, Hideki has a logistics problem. He has a killer, a corpse, and a guy passed out. He also has three cars. How to set the scene so it looks like Aoki did it?

"He puts the detective in his car —"

"Whose car?"

"The detective's car. He drives him to the Tastee Freez, dumps the body out back, and leaves the car out front. He puts the puzzle and the sudoku on the sword, sticks it back in the wound, wraps the guy's fingers around it, and walks the half a mile to where he's left his car.

"The stage is set to frame Aoki. There's only one problem. Since the sword is the one Dennis stole from the antique shop, and since Dennis is still alive, he has to be very careful the police don't think Dennis did it.

"How does he do that? Easy. He opens the door of Dennis's car and smears blood on his hands. *Without* blood on his hands, Dennis could have committed the crime, *not* gotten bloody, driven away, and passed out. But there's no way he committed the crime, got bloody, then drove the car half a mile without messing it up. Blood on Dennis, but none on the steering wheel, is proof conclusive he didn't do it.

"Which is exactly what Hideki wants.

"It also serves another purpose. Hideki wants to frame Aoki by making it look like Aoki framed him. How was Aoki framing him? By leaving his Social Security number. But Aoki can't possibly believe that won't be seen through as a hollow sham. Because why would Hideki leave his own number?

"So, here we get into triple-think. It will look like Aoki also framed Dennis, in an obvious way that's easily seen through, to mask the actual frame he was making on Hideki."

"I'm getting a terrible headache," Harper said. "How the hell am I going to prove any of that?"

"You don't need to. That's the beauty of it. Hideki slipped up in court. His ass is grass. These are arguments his lawyer will have to deal with."

"Whoever that poor fellow is," Harper said, "I don't envy him his job."

"Never mind the permutations and convolutions of this plot. The bottom line is Hideki killed the guy, and Hideki put the sudoku and the crossword on the samurai sword."

"That's right," Harper said. "No one else put them there."

Cora frowned. "Why do you say that?"

Chief Harper tipped back in his desk chair, scratched his head. "The day of the murder, you left your purse in my office."

"Yeah. I guess I was excited."

"I guess you were. But not so excited you couldn't solve the puzzle once I faxed it to you."

"What are you getting at?"

"Nothing," Harper said. "It's just things get left in my office all the time. When that happens, you have to identify them, call the person who left them, ask them to pick 'em up."

"Which you did."

"Yeah," Harper said. "Which I did. And now you tell me this story about cars, and swords, and puzzles. And it's so complicated. Requires so much expertise."

"Please. You're giving me a swelled head."

"It also puzzling. I hate to use that word. But it's hard to figure out. And I have to wonder."

Chief Harper picked up a stapler from his desk. Seemed to find it fascinating. Fiddled with it while he spoke. "Just for the sake of argument, suppose I looked in your purse, to see whose it was, and found a puzzle. And suppose it happened to be the same one found on the body. Except it was already solved. That would be rather strange, wouldn't it?"

Cora eyed Chief Harper narrowly. "It certainly would."

"Particularly with the puzzle getting torn off the sword and all. And you finding it in the woods. That would be enough to make one think."

"Think what, Chief?"

"Oh, I don't know. Of the various legal statutes involved. Tampering with evidence. Suppressing evidence. Failure to report a crime. It could be quite a mess."

"Sounds like it could."

Harper studied the stapler, shook his head. "I don't know what I would have done."

Cora shrugged and smiled.

"Good thing you didn't look in my purse."

ABOUT THE AUTHOR

Edgar, Shamus, and Lefty nominee **Parnell Hall** is the author of the Puzzle Lady crossword puzzle mysteries, the Stanley Hastings private eye novels, and the Steve Winslow courtroom dramas. An actor, screenwriter, and former private investigator, Parnell lives in New York City. Visit his Web site at www.parnellhall.com.